# SPELL OVER TROUBLED WATER

*Grimoires of a Middle-aged Witch Book 4*

## RENEE GEORGE

Barkside of the Moon Press

Spell Over Troubled Water

Grimoires of a Middle-aged Witch Book 4

Publisher: Barkside of the Moon Press

Print ISBN: 978-1-947177-45-1

*For Ashton*

# ACKNOWLEDGMENTS

I have to thank the usual people for helping me get to the end of this book.

First, Robyn Peterman and Robbin Clubb, my critique partners, who know just when to kick my ass when I need it! Thank you, Lindas!

Second, to the readers and my Rebels, without you all, what would be the point? I am so happy and blessed to have you guys in my corner!

Third, thank you, Mitra! You know why.

Forth, but not least, coffee. Thank you strong black coffee, for giving me the energy to bring this baby home. You are the miracle in my life.

**Being a forty-something, newly divorced, single mom is getting easier every day. Thankfully, so is being a witch, you know, when monsters and power-hungry sorcerers aren't trying to kill me. And they aren't the only ones who want to take me down. Too bad for all of them. I don't die easy.**

Now that my nero-craft has been triggered, I'm off to the Iron Grove compound, along with my hot druid boyfriend and his violently awesome sister, to learn magic from the best of the best. Of course, not every druid or tru-craft witch is happy about me adding water magic to the earth, fire, and air magic I already wield. There is even talk of a test they want me to take that sounds about as much fun as an alien probing. No, thank you.

I'll have to rely on allies, old and new if I want to survive the incoming tide of enemies who want me to drown in my own magic.

Literally.

# CHAPTER 1

THE FEEL OF KEIR'S BODY WHEN HE SHOVED ME against the padded wall of the gym at Iron Grove quickened my pulse. I shivered with delicious anticipation as he held my wrists above my head, then dipped his lips to my ear.

"Calm," he whispered.

I tried to yank myself out of his hold, but his sinewy muscles were stronger than my own. My breath came in short pants as sweat beaded my brow. "Don't you know you should never tell a woman to calm down?"

"Adrenaline will get you killed in hand-to-hand combat," he said. "You have to learn to calm...uhm, I mean, you have to find a way to keep your fight or flight reflexes in check. You're getting too excited."

I leaned in and gave his neck a playful nip. I felt his pulse leap under my tongue. I smiled. "I'm not the only one excited."

"Yeah," he rasped. "But this isn't a fight."

"I don't think any bad guys are planning to kiss me to death."

Keir chuckled. "Maybe we should take a break."

He stole my rebuttal with a kiss that left me breathless and weak in the knees. He shifted his hips against me as he moved his mouth over mine. My fingers itched to touch him, but he held my wrists firm. His tongue slipped past my parted lips. His touch electrified my body and stole my will to resist. His kiss became insistent, hungry, and possessive as I went up on my toes to meet his passion with my own. Our bond transcended the physical. Until Keir, I'd never understood "I'd die for you."

I moaned.

Keir moaned.

Luanne, Keir's sister, also moaned. "Dudes," she complained. "We're supposed to be training Iris in hand-to-hand combat, not auditioning her for a porno."

I giggled.

Keir quirked a brow at me and grinned. "Spoilsport," he muttered before stepping back and letting my wrists go. He turned to Lu. "Sorry." He gave her a two-finger salute. "Back to it, Drill Sergeant."

"Har, har," she replied. "If I was a drill sergeant, you'd be dropping and giving me a hundred right now."

"A hundred what?" I asked her. "If it's dollars, I'll happily pay the price to end this session early."

"You wish," Lu scoffed.

I really did. When we arrived at Iron Grove to meet Archdruid Freya and her bonded witch Thomas, I'd been super stoked. Then we were told that they'd been called away on "business," and we'd been instructed to stay put until they returned. This made me understandably less stoked. That had been three days ago.

As a result of all the free time on our hands, both Keir and Lu insisted that I brush up on self-defense. *Blech*. I was better at the physical stuff since taking my sister Rose's hard-core Cross-fit sessions, but I still didn't love working out. Still, learning to be a better fighter probably wasn't a bad idea. I'd be the first to admit that my magic didn't always work the way I wanted it to, so having a backup plan was smart. I just didn't relish all the residual aches and pains that went along with it. I wanted to be at my best when I met Thomas. I was eager to learn from the old tru-crafter, and I hoped he could help me focus my magic in a way that didn't involve me dying a horrible death.

It had been a week since I'd purposely activated nero-craft, and so far, I'd not been able to perform a single spell. Reflecting back, I'd been full of hubris when I'd rubbed my spit on my grimoire. After I'd finally managed to wrangle air magic, I'd really thought I'd discovered the key to all tru-craft. But so far, I hadn't been able to do anything with water that didn't involve employing earth, fire, and air.

Keir told me to be patient, but I had to constantly fight to keep the panic to a minimum. I'd nearly died learning my first element, tera-craft. It had taken weeks for ignis-craft to flare to life. Aero-craft had taken hold within a few days, but it had been unstable as all get-out. I was determined to embrace nero-craft. To face it without fear or apprehension whenever it chose to rear its watery head.

I had been excited to go to Iron Grove, but now that I was hundreds of miles from home in a remote location in Northern Michigan, I missed my kid, Linda the Gnome, and Bob the butthole-less imp.

"When do you think Thomas and your grandmother will get back?" I asked as we lined up for our next go-around.

Lu made an annoyed sound. She had a big bug up her butt about her grandmother. She blamed the woman for her beloved grandfather's death. The fact that Keir didn't share Lu's animosity toward the powerful duo made me wonder if Lu's anger was a case of misplaced grief.

A man with platinum blond hair and dark brown eyes, wearing gray workout gear and holding a duffel bag, knocked outside the room before he entered. I'd met him earlier in the week. Lu had introduced him as Simon, one of a dozen druids tasked with guarding the Iron Grove. His gaze shifted around the room to take in the scene. He raised his brows. "They're back," he said. "The Archdruid wants all three of you to join her for dinner."

"And people in Hell want ice cream," Lu replied. "You can tell her eminence that it's a hard pass from me."

Simon made a noise of dissent and shook his head. "Tell her yourself at dinner." He didn't wait around to listen to the onslaught of curses that came rapid-fire from Lu.

I placed my hands on Keir's shoulders. "It's showtime."

I DON'T KNOW what I'd expected when I found out we were having dinner in the archdruid's quarters, but a rectangular farmhouse-style table with mismatched chairs in a large cozy kitchen hadn't been on my archdruid bingo card. Even with the window open and a fresh breeze coming in, the savory scent of roasted carrots, onions, and cooking wine filled the space and made my mouth water. Freya Quinn was a tall, slender woman. She had a mass of frizzy gray hair that spilled down her back. Her eyes were gray, reminiscent of tumbled smoky quartz, and her gaze was sharp, clear, and shrewd. I imagined she didn't miss much. Some people equated being old with being frail. There was nothing frail about the archdruid.

She smiled as she greeted us. "Keir, my darling." She held out her arms. "I've missed you."

"Mam-o." Keir embraced the older woman and kissed her cheek. "It's good to see you."

"Where's your sister?" she asked as they parted.

"You know Lu," Keir said. I smiled when he reached back and held his hand out to me. "This is Iris."

The woman gave me an assessing look and then nodded. "We finally meet."

"It's a pleasure, Archdruid." I did an awkward half-curtsy, half-nod, with a two-finger salute as I searched for a hole to crawl inside. I was making a terrible first impression.

The archdruid's eyes widened, and her frown deepened. Then, she started to laugh. "Oh, my dear girl. There is no need for such formality. Please, call me Freya." She gestured to a covered Dutch oven on the stove. "I've made coq au vin."

"You made it?" I asked, unable to keep the incredulity from my voice. "I mean. I didn't expect...."

"Mam-o makes a mean coq au vin." Keir walked over to the stove and tipped the lid up on the pot. "Damn, that smells great. You're going to love it." He smiled at his grandmother. "My mouth is watering already."

Mam-o smacked his hand before he could dip his finger into the sauce. "Wash your hands and have a seat."

Keir and I went to the sink and washed up. He handed me a hand towel to dry with. As I patted my hands, I asked, "Can I help you with anything?"

"No," Keir said quick enough to give me whiplash. He grinned sheepishly. "No offense, but you're better at potions than you are at—"

I raised my hand to stop him. "I wasn't offering to cook, just help." He looked so relieved I was a little wounded. "I make a mean mac-and-cheese."

"With cut-up smoked sausages," he added. "I remember. It was...edible."

I flicked his shoulder. "Hey, that's Michael's favorite."

He rubbed the spot and chuckled. "Maybe when he was seven."

It was hard to defend mac-n-meat, but I tried anyhow. "I elevated the dish by not using hot dogs."

Keir grinned. "Lucky me."

My lip curled into a snarl, and I bared my teeth. "Not tonight, you're not."

"Behave, children." The archdruid took the coq au vin from the stove and set it on the table. "Now sit."

The table had four settings, including plates, napkins, forks, and butter knives. Freya retrieved a boule of bread from the oven and set it down next to the pot. I took the chair closest to the entry. "Is Thomas joining us?" Keir sat in the seat next to me.

"Our trip was taxing, and he was eager to get home." She took the lid off and slipped a ladle inside. "He'll meet you tomorrow."

Keir held out his plate as she served him a helping of the chicken and veggie dish.

"Taxing, huh? Anything you can talk about?" he asked.

She ladled a serving of the savory chicken dish onto my plate and gave me a tight smile. "That's why I invited you both to dinner."

Keir's brows narrowed. "Was your trip about Iris?"

"Me?" I stopped salivating and gave the woman a sharp look. "Why would it be about me?"

"Unfortunately, word gets around," Freya said. "The North American Council of Groves found out that you can command multiple elements."

"Who told them?" I asked.

"Word has a way of traveling in our world." Freya waved her hand as if to clear the air, then sat in the chair to my left. "The point is, the other groves know about you now."

"Okay." I took a bite, and it was heaven. "Damn, this is so good." I wagged my fork at her. "Did you put peaches in this?"

"Close." She gave me a nod of approval. "You're tasting the chantarelles."

"Mushrooms?" I'd heard of chantarelles, but I don't think I'd ever eaten them before.

"Yes." Her gray eyes brightened. "They give a slight fruitiness to the dish without adding sweetness."

"Genius." I took another bite.

"Can we stay on topic?" Keir asked. I heard the concern in his voice and knew he was worried.

Freya sighed. "Representatives from all the North American groves and their tru-craft covens are coming to witness Iris's test."

I paused between bites. "Ugh. I am not a good test taker." I paused, my fork aimed at a tender piece of juicy chicken. "What kind of test?"

"There will be four challenges that you will have to master using cunning, craft, and control." She kept her gaze steady on me as she added, "It's an ancient rite of passage for tru-craft witches called the *malificionito*."

"No." Keir stood up, anger hardening his eyes. "Not the *malificionito*."

"From what you've said, Iris is strong. She'll be fine." Freya wouldn't make eye contact. That made me nervous. She didn't strike me as a woman cowed by truth.

"Every time people start throwing around foreign words, I'm worried. What's this *maleficent*, and why is it *neat-o*?"

"*Malificionito*," Freya corrected. "It's an ancient test designed to weed out false witches."

"I'm not a false witch."

"It doesn't matter," said Keir, his voice tight with anger. "Anyone claiming to possess tru-craft can be tested in the *malificionito*. They have to face a single trial for the element they claim. Pretenders died."

I gave him a sharp look. "And the real deals?"

"They sometimes died as well." Keir glared at his grandmother. "The test can push your magic to the point of burn."

"Aether dust?" I asked.

Keir nodded. "Aether dust."

Okay, that was bad. Aether dust was a result of magic burning so hot the unfortunate witch would feel like she was puking and crapping solar flares until her flesh and bones disintegrated into magical ash. I'd felt this way when earth magic nearly killed me, and I had no desire to suffer through it again. I wouldn't risk my life just to prove to a bunch of bitchy witches that I possessed tru-craft.

"I don't need to prove my witch-worthiness," I said. "So that's a maleficent-no."

Freya looked at me, her expression grim. "I'm sorry, Iris. You don't have a choice."

# CHAPTER 2

Blindsided. That was the only word to describe how I felt. I'd come to the Iron Grove compound in good faith. This was supposed to be a simple face-to-face introduction to Freya and Thomas. I'd hoped to learn more about tru-craft while I was here and, maybe, unlock some of the secrets to my past. But being forced into taking an ancient witch-killing test? Wow. I had not seen that coming.

"She said no." Keir stood up and dropped his napkin onto his still-full plate. "We're leaving."

A tell-tale tingle started in my lips and tongue as my peripheral vision dimmed. I grabbed the edge of the table and took two sharp, quick breaths to clear my head. Passing out face-first in the archdruid's coq au vin wasn't an option.

"Keir, you know how this works," said Freya. "The council voted, and we must abide by the ruling."

"Iris is not a member of the Grove," said Keir. "She doesn't have to abide by their archaic rules."

"If the decision was mine, I would outlaw the *malifi-cionito*. Thomas and I stopped the practice in our territories. But it remains an option in other Groves, and unfortunately, the majority of the Council voted for the *malificionito*."

"Obviously," I muttered as the light-headedness cleared and I found my legs. I stood up from the table. Keir's face was a mire of anger, confusion, and betrayal, but even more, I saw fear. Whatever these tests were, they frightened him. He was scared I couldn't survive. Freya gestured to the chairs. "Please, sit back down, you two." Keir scoffed. "Goodbye, Archdruid Quinn." He grasped my arm and tugged me toward the door.

"Iris, the Council doesn't believe that you're faking tru-craft. They want to test you to see if you can control your powers."

Keir and I stopped and turned once again to face the archdruid. "I can control my magic," I protested.

"Barely," she said. "Trust me, Iris. The *malificionito* is the lesser of two evils."

"What do you mean?" Keir asked. He crossed his arms over his chest. "Five minutes, Mam-o. Then we leave."

I nodded to the older woman. "What he said."

"But we're not sitting," he added.

"Stubborn children," Freya said. "Sit or don't sit. It won't make any difference in the telling."

Freya might look like a hippy, artsy, kind and cool grandmother, but you didn't get to be archdruid without some serious mojo. If she thought the *malificionito* was the least evil, what the heck was the other option?

Freya pinned her gaze to mine. "The Council is understandably worried. Your inability to regulate your tru-craft magic has resulted in real-world consequences. For example, you called up a powerful god-like creature and almost destroyed an entire mountain."

"In my defense, I didn't call him, he came all on his own, and I did manage to defeat the jerk and save the mountain."

"You started a pixie mating ritual several centuries early and endangered humans by fighting multiple magical creatures."

"To protect the pixies," I said. "It all worked out in the end. And the queen named her baby after me."

Freya pinched the bridge of her nose and closed her eyes for a moment before meeting my gaze. "They wanted to bind your magic, Iris. But the Green Grove leader, Derrick Asher, suggested the *malificionito*. I seconded the motion to prevent the greater injustice. Luckily, the vote passed four to two, with dissent from the Bezoar and Luna groves."

Keir told me that Iron Grove ruled the North American druids. "But aren't you the head druid, the arch over all the arches? Can't you just tell them to go to Hell and be done with it?"

Freya gave me a sad smile and shook her head. "I'm afraid the Iron Grove wouldn't be in charge for long if I didn't give the other groves some say in the way we govern our kind. Including having a voice in this decision. It's a great way to incite a rebellion, and I've already lost too much to the last civil war."

An empty pit of despair formed in my gut.

Three months ago, I might have gotten in line for the

binding train. Magic had been nothing but trouble in the beginning. If I was being honest, it still had its challenges. But I loved my life, mountain-destroying gods and all. I couldn't imagine a world without Linda the gnome, or Bob, my cuddly butthole-less imp. I glanced at Keir. He was my soulmate. If it wasn't for magic, I wouldn't have him in my life. Truth be told, I love being a tru-craft witch. I didn't want to lose that part of me. The pit in my stomach grew sickeningly large.

"The bottom line," said Freya, "is that if you don't participate in the *malificionito* and prove you can control the elements, the Council will bind your magic."

"They can't." I shook my head. "I won't allow it."

"Iris," Keir said, his voice tense. "Your hands."

I looked at him, then down at my fingers. They were dripping with flames that licked the tiled floor. Crap. So much for my self-control. I clenched my fist and extinguished the fire. I didn't need to give the druids more reason to cut me off from my powers.

"The *malificionito* is your best option for a positive outcome," said Freya.

"As long as I don't die. I mean, those are my choices, right? Have my powers taken away or risk getting killed."

"It won't be easy, but you are no ordinary witch. I believe you can and will survive."

"When is the test?" asked Keir.

"The Council will be here tomorrow. The challenges will begin two nights hence." "That's the autumnal equinox," Keir said. "When the sun crosses the celestial divide, her magic will be super-powered."

"Extra magic is good, right?" I asked.

"It will make your tru-craft...unpredictable."

"So, the opposite of good." I turned my gaze to Freya. "Two nights from now isn't good for me. Let's schedule for some time next month." I said it like a joke, but I was deadly serious. I knew what my magic would do to me if it went wild. Poof. Dust.

Freya shook her head. "I'm sorry, Iris. They know you possess a fourth element, and the Council worries about your magical aptitude."

"Mam-o, did you tell the Council about Iris's nerocraft?"

"You told them? What? How?" I cast an accusing glare at Keir. I knew he had to report to his people, but he told me that he didn't tell them everything.

He shook his head. "It wasn't me."

There was only one more person I could think of who I interacted with regularly and who had ties to the grove. It hurt to think she might have betrayed me. She was like a sister now. Chosen family. I'd made her part of my coven. Would she have ratted me out? It didn't sound like the druid-warrior I knew and loved, but I still had to ask. "Luanne?"

"It wasn't either of my grandchildren." Her expression wasn't happy. "Thomas told me."

"The rat-fink," I muttered. I'd forgotten that I'd mentioned triggering the water symbol in the grimoire to him, but I'd expected his discretion.

"We're bonded," Freya said. "He could no more keep it from me than you could keep a similar secret from Keir."

I sighed. It had been naive of me to assume Thomas would keep our conversations to himself. But what did it matter? "Well, my water magic hasn't sparked yet." So far, it had been a big fat drought when it came to nero-craft. "So, I've only mastered three of the elements."

If I was being honest, mastering was a strong word when it came to magic. My level of witchcraft was on the shy side of adequate.

Freya's gaze met mine. "I think that's part of what's got the council worried."

There was still something I didn't understand about the situation. "I get why Thomas told you about the nero-craft, but if neither of you told the council, then how did they find out?"

"They had already been informed before I arrived," she admitted.

Keir's jaw flexed. "By whom?"

Freya shrugged. "I wish I knew. As it stands, I'm afraid we have a mole in the Iron Grove."

# CHAPTER 3

When we got back to our room, a big orange floof was stretched out on the bed.

"Bob!" Tears clouded my vision as I raced to my loveable, cuddly imp. The moment I scooped him into my arms, he began to purr. I could feel the stress melt from me. I glanced up at Keir, his expression tight with worry. "How did he get here?"

"Imps are mysterious creatures." He smiled. "He sensed you needed him."

I hugged Bob tighter. "I really did."

"I'm not well versed in the *malificionito*. And the Harvest Moon will magnify your magic, so we don't know what to expect. I'm going to the library to do some research."

Reluctantly, I set Bob aside. He plopped back down on the bed with a snort and an adorable sneeze. As bad as I felt, I couldn't stop the smile tugging at my lips. Bob really was like diazepam, chamomile tea, and cookie dough ice cream rolled up into a warm fuzzy hug.

I wrapped my arms around Keir's waist. "If researching is what you need to do, then go do it. As the old saying goes, we have a long way to go and a short time to get there. Get to getting."

"The old stories of the *malificionito* aren't good, Iris. More people die than survive. Maybe we should pack up and leave."

I shook my head. "A life on the run? No, thanks. My son is in his senior year of school. My family finally knows about my secret witch life. And I love living in Southill Village. Besides, I'm the only one who can protect the town and my family when things get magical."

"You're my world, Iris, and our bond makes me feel crazy sometimes. Especially when you put other people before yourself."

"You put me before yourself all the time."

"It's as natural as breathing for me," he replied.

Divine intervention, if you believed in that sort of thing, solidified our partnership in the womb. But the bond between us was unequal, magically designed that way—probably by the same idiot who devised the *malificionito*. I knew I was the most important thing in Keir's world. I loved him with every cell in my body. It would kill me if anything happened to him. But, if a bus was barreling toward him and Michael, and I could only save one of them, I'd pick my son. Keir understood that he wasn't number one, and he didn't hold it against me. But now wasn't the time for lamenting. I had to pass the biggest final exam of my life because failure meant death.

He kissed me. "Hopefully, the archives will hold a

nugget of wisdom that will give us a strong chance of succeeding."

I hugged him again. "I'll keep the good juju that you find wisdom nuggets, then."

"You should get some rest. We'll have a lot to do tomorrow to prepare you."

"You got it. Go." I kissed the tip of his nose. "Use that big, beautiful brain of yours to find out what we need to know."

His smile widened. "I love you."

"I love you back." I slid my hands down his back and patted his ass. "Do your thing."

"You're my thing."

I laughed. "Do your other thing, and then come back and do me."

"Deal."

I let him go, and he left the room. My imagination took me through dozens of scary scenarios, all of them ending with me turning to aether dust. Worrying didn't bring solutions, so Keir's research was my best shot at survival.

Bob, who'd jumped down from the bed, weaved his body between my legs. I held back the sob threatening to choke me. "Nope," I told the imp. "Not going to do it. I've faced worse situations in the past several months, and these tests can't be any worse, right?"

Bob let out a quick *myip* sound, then rubbed his face against my calves as he continued to purr. I'd left my phone in our room to charge and retrieved it from the bedside table. Two missed calls and a text. The calls were from my sister Marigold with no voicemails. The text was from Michael.

*Dad is here. Can he stay at the house?*

I typed out, "No. Our home isn't his hotel." I paused before pressing send. I thought of the house as mine now, and I had erased Evan's presence with the angry thoroughness of a wife scorned. But now? I had Keir. I had a new life. And I was a freaking witch. More than all that, Michael was finally in a good place with his dad. He'd been angry with Evan for a long time for having an affair with the football coach and breaking up our family. It had taken a year of counseling for him to forgive and heal. I wouldn't undo all that emotional growth with one angry text.

I deleted my first response, then texted, *fine.*

Being an adult was hard.

I hit send, then called Marigold back.

"Hey, Iris," she said when she answered. "Have you talked to Michael?"

"Sorta. He texted and asked me if his dad could stay at the house. Is the motel all booked up?"

"Michael thought because you weren't home, you wouldn't mind Evan hanging out there for a couple of days."

"Honestly, I don't want Evan breathing all over the house." After my ex moved out, I completely redid the bedroom. Without a cheapskate husband to shoot down every expenditure, I'd finally bought the deluxe mattress I'd always wanted. I put Marigold on speaker, then quickly texted Michael.

*He can sleep on the couch.*

I got two thumbs-up emojis in reply.

"Why is he in Southill? Oh my God, did Adam kick him to the curb?" My stomach dipped at the thought of Evan never leaving my house again. He'd be there, moping and eating all the ice cream and lamenting his broken heart. Seeking comfort from the wife he dumped...really? Oh, the irony.

"The opposite of breaking up, actually," Marigold said. "Evan and Adam are getting married. He wanted to tell Michael in person."

"Um, he could've mentioned that to me before telling Michael. Do I need to come home?"

"Nah. If there's anything that kid of yours has proven over the last few months, it's that he's resilient. He takes after his mom."

"So, he's doing okay?"

"He's handling the news well," Marigold told me. "You raised a capable young man, Iris."

I knew that it was down to Michael's own character and personality more than anything I'd done. I'd gotten lucky in the son department, and I didn't take it for granted. Still, Marigold's praise made me feel good. "Thanks." After a reflective pause, I asked, "Are you at the house now?"

"Yep. Evan called me while he was on the way to town, so I came over to support Michael. Turned out to be a big-nothing burger. I didn't want to leave without talking to you first."

"Hence the two missed calls."

"Hence," she agreed. Marigold's voice lowered., "I'm in the garden, and I'm not alone."

"Is a grouchy rock-throwing gnome nearby?"

"Yes. And she wants to know when you're coming home."

"I'm not sure. There have been some...complications."

"That doesn't sound good."

In the background, I heard Linda say, "What has the ignorant *Kleinkind* done now?"

I fought the urge to duck. "Tell her I didn't *do* anything. I'm just out here trying to live my best life, and there are forces at work trying to make it impossible."

"What's going on, Iris?" I heard the worry in Marigold's voice. "How bad is it?"

"There was a big meeting between all the PICs."

"P. I. C.?"

"Pricks-In-Charge."

"Ah. Go on."

"They've decided amongst themselves that I can't be trusted with my magic. They want to bind my power."

I heard a string of Germanic cuss words in the background.

"They can't do that," Marigold protested.

I sat on the bed, flopped back, and let out an exasperated sigh. "It turns out it's an actual thing."

"But you can stop them, right?"

"Well, if I pass this test of theirs, then yes."

"You've always been great with tests," she said. "Wait a minute." She was no longer talking to me. "Uh, huh," I heard her say, followed by an "Okay."

"Everything all right?" I asked.

"Evan wants to talk to you," Marigold said.

I frowned at the request, but managed to keep my tone neutral. "Why?"

"I can tell him to piss off," she told me. I heard a grunt of protest from my ex.

I chuckled as I considered her offer. "Nah. Put him on."

"Iris," Evan said, his tone smooth. "Thanks for letting me crash at the house."

"On the couch," I remarked.

"Of course. On the couch. I, uh, was hoping you'd be home so we could talk."

"You're marrying Adam. Congrats."

"Um, thanks." He sounded nervous.

"Nice chat," I told him. "Give the phone back to Marigold."

"That's it?" asked Evan. "You don't want to yell at me or anything?"

"Nope. It's all good."

"Iris, I know you well enough to know that *all good* means *go to hell.*"

"Well, it's not the ideal honeymoon spot, but I hear the Lake of Fire is magnificent this time of year."

"And there it is," said Evan. "Does sarcasm make you feel better?"

"Immensely. Did you need anything else?"

"Michael said you were meeting Keir's grandmother for the first time."

Thank you, Michael. Ugh. "Yep. That's true enough."

"Meeting the family is a big step. So...are things serious between you two?"

"What are you, my dad? You're not part of my life

anymore, Evan. Our connection is Michael, and that's it. Go spend time with your son. He's missed you."

I hung up before he could respond. Evan loved controlling the narrative when it came to our relationship. I'd been mad at him for a long time, but my anger had mostly faded. I'd made being Evan's wife my full-time job for too many years, and because of that, I'd lost sight of who I was. Keir, for all his protectiveness, didn't try to control and manipulate me.

Bob lay down next to me, his warm, fuzzy body vibrating against my arm. "Bob, you are the best." My phone beeped—a text from Marigold. *Call me if you need me to unload a can of whoop ass. I got your back, front, and both sides.*

Her message made me smile. Marigold was my sister, but she was also my best friend, and I knew without a doubt she'd take on any danger to protect me. In the last few months, that meant danger of the supernatural variety, and she'd done it with barely a blink.

I was glad she was back in Southill with Michael because I knew she'd protect him the same way.

There was a knock at the door.

"Yep," I said loudly.

Luanne opened the door and popped her head in. "You up for a distraction?" she asked.

I sat up. "Oh, God, yes."

# CHAPTER 4

"How many halls does this place have?" I followed Lu down a fourth passage and into another stairwell. "And why are there so many stairs?"

"It's a four-story forty-thousand square foot mega-mansion," she said with a shrug. "It's bound to have a lot of halls and stairs."

"This place has to be worth what? Six million? Seven million dollars? It seems like someone could've sprung for an elevator."

"I think they bought it for one-point-eight million in nineteen-sixty-two. It would probably list at twenty or thirty million now."

"Wow." I gave a low whistle. "The taxes and insurance have got to be massive."

Lu stopped and arched her brow at me. "

"Druidry is a legally recognized religion. The grove is exempted from a lot of taxes."

I rolled my eyes. "Still, it's got to be expensive to keep the lights on."

"That's above my paygrade." She waved me forward. "Come on."

"I'm definitely getting my steps in."

Lu chuckled. "Rose would be so proud."

Rose, my youngest sister, a cross-fit fanatic and health nut, had taken on the role of my personal trainer. She took an immense amount of pleasure in torturing me. "I know I said I wanted a distraction, but...."

"Stop complaining. I am taking you on an adventure."

"You're being so secretive."

"I don't want to spoil the surprise."

"I'm not really a surprise kind of gal," I said. "They never lead anywhere good."

"This will be an exception," she promised with a sly grin.

As we headed down another set of stairs, I deeply regretted leaving Bob and the comfort of my room.

It was dark when we exited through a door at the bottom of the steps, and I was surprised when a brisk breeze blew up my shirt. "Whew!"

"That happens because the hedge maze funnels wind toward the house into this patio area."

"Hedge maze?" My eyes widened. "Way to bury the lead. Has there been a maze here the whole time, and you're just now telling me about it?"

"I knew you'd love it, but that's not the whole surprise."

"Tell me?"

"Find your way through the maze and find out," she teased.

"You're killing me."

"It's worth it, I promise."

I rolled my eyes, but I couldn't stop smiling. "Fine," I said. "But there better not be a minotaur at the center of this labyrinth."

She lightly punched my arm. "Afraid I'm going to make you a sacrifice?"

"I wasn't...." I let the implication hang.

Lu gave me a shove into the maze. "You first."

"But—"

"The maze is a series of concentric circles with a lot of openings that lead to dead ends and only one way that will take you to the center. Our destination. I know the path well and could lead you there, but what fun would that be?"

Honestly, it felt good to solve a problem that didn't have dire consequences if I made the wrong decision. Luanne had asked me if I wanted a distraction. Well, distraction-level had been achieved. I turned back and gave her a nod. Challenge accepted.

The hedge row that made up the maze was at least seven or eight feet tall. Way over my head. The moon was nearly full tonight but not directly overhead, which meant the maze was steeped in shadows.

We were traveling left, so I reached out to the hedges on my right, then tripped on an exposed root in the pathway and stumbled forward. "Crap. I can't see a thing."

"Your eyes will adjust," Lu said. "Just give it time."

"Or I could try a little spell."

"Go for it. Just don't destroy the garden," she teased.

"You're hilarious." About a foot above my head, I saw

a firefly dancing in the maze above me. I pinched the air below it between my forefinger and thumb. "*Air is fair to capture a sprite. Ignite the light. Blow and glow. Make it bright.*" I focused on bending the wind into an egg shape around the firefly. "Blow and glow," I coaxed. To my immense joy and pride, the egg of light with only a single firefly inside illuminated the area around me.

"Nifty," Lu said, clearly impressed.

"Fair Konig showed me how to do it." The pixie king had been coaching me on using air elements without conjuring up tornadoes or losing myself in the process, and he'd been doing it without throwing a single object at my head.

Lu stared at my makeshift lantern. "But fireflies don't actually generate light, right? I mean, they just glow in the dark."

"*Actually*, they do generate light." The firefly flashed its tail as if to agree. "They produce a chemical called luciferin, and an enzyme luciferase that when combined with oxygen acts as a fuel that causes them to light up."

"That's *actually* pretty cool."

"Thank you."

"Does the container harm the bug?"

"No," I told her. "It can breathe inside the egg, and when we reach our destination, I'll let it go."

She gave me a grudging nod of respect. "Again. Very cool."

The maze had a distinct resinous scent, almost like a clipped evergreen but not as crisp. I used my will to push the spelled light ahead of us as we made quick work moving through row after row, occasionally meeting dead ends and retracing our steps. Luanne laughed every time. I found the challenging puzzle exhilarating.

Four rings in, I heard a faint lyrical hum. "What's that?"

"Keep going and find out."

"You're not giving anything away, are you?"

She smirked. "Nope."

We kept going, but it didn't take long before I turned the final corner into the interior circle. "Oh my."

"Told you," Lu said with satisfaction. "Worth it?"

I let out a slow breath, then said, "Definitely." A mini-Stonehenge had been built in the middle of the maze. At its direct center was a stone altar. Six people in black robes surrounded the altar, and they were chanting a song in a language I didn't understand. The humming I'd heard in the previous row.

"Fly free, little firefly," I said quietly, and I released our guide back into the maze.

The altar had green and gold candles in all four corners. From my studies, I knew that green candles were used in earth magic and yellow symbolized air and the sun. I wasn't sure if the same meanings were attached to druidic rituals.

The flickering flames created a dance of light over a tall iridescent jug with a narrow-fluted opening and a generous lip. The jug was surrounded by what looked like eight matching mortar vessels. There was a tray of figs, grapes, cherries, and an assortment of nuts on the surface, as well. The robed druids joined their hands and lifted them to the sky as they continued their melody.

"Are we allowed to be here?" I asked Luanne.

Lu nodded. "Yes." Her tone had taken on a hushed "in-church" quality, so I followed her example. "What are they doing?"

She leaned to my ear and said, "They're practicing for a choir competition."

I whipped my gaze to her. "Seriously."

Lu snickered. "Not hardly." She shook her head and grinned. "This is a *canticum* to the goddess Braciaca for a good harvest."

"Like for the Harvest Moon? I thought that wasn't for a few days."

"No, this is for all the farmers in our territory. Mostly in the Midwest. They harvest through September, so the ceremony is performed on a weekly basis until the farmers are done."

"You guys ask your goddess to bless the harvest for people you don't know. Why?"

"Because a good harvest benefits everyone, not just people who all believe the same way." She gave me a "duh" look.

We moved closer to the druids, and the singing became louder.

"How is that possible? I could barely hear them before. Did they get louder when we came through?"

"No," Lu said. "It's the way the henge works. It amplifies the voices inside the circle, but it also acts as a sound barrier so that it keeps the sound in by bouncing it around the pillars."

"Why? The primitive science behind the unique acoustics is fascinating, but does it serve a more practical purpose?"

Luanne smiled and gestured toward the sky. "To carry our songs of prayers to our gods and goddesses, of course."

"Are your deities in the clouds?"

"They are all around us. They live in and around every believer."

I never talked about Druidry with Lu. Based on her devil-may-care attitude and devotion to sarcasm and violence, I'd naturally assumed she wasn't very religious. The reverence in her tone surprised me.

"Is that what the druids in the circle are doing? Praying?" I'd only known about druids, witches, and the supernatural world for a little over three months. I'd been so focused on learning how to manage magic and not die that I hadn't considered what it meant to be a druid. "Is that where you get your...abilities from?"

"It's more complicated than that, but it's not far off the mark. Our connection to our gods and goddesses is in our DNA. We can feel them from the moment we draw breath."

Her explanation reminded me a little of what Keir had said he'd felt the moment I'd been born. It was hard to reconcile the little I knew about druid culture and lineage with what I knew about Keir and Luanne. Until I met them, I'd always thought a druid was something you became, not something you inherited. "Are all druids born druid?"

She smiled. "Not all. There are several different kinds of druids in the world, just like witches. Not all witches are tru-craft."

Keir had explained that to me when I first found out

about my powers. There were types of witches who were born, like tru-crafters. Some made, like sorcerers, and some who sought out the practice, like Wiccans. All very different but still very real. "What kind of druids are you?"

"We are the *Kurisa-sa*. The people of the red mountain. Our kind predates any written language, and there is archeological evidence of our kin going back to 26,000 B.C."

I let out a low whistle. "That's a long time."

Lu chuckled. "It sure is. I won't get into all the sacrifices, human and animal alike."

I pressed my hand to my chest. "That's not—"

"They put an end to living sacrifices thousands of years ago, but it was pretty common practice in ancient times." She rolled her eyes. "Don't tell Keir I told you about that. He likes to pretend we're above that kind of behavior."

I frowned. "Well, I think Bogmall is a prime example of the fact that human sacrifice isn't that far in the past." After all, the druid-turned-sorcerer had tried to gut me on a stone altar to rob me of my magic and take it for herself.

"Truth," Lu agreed. As the song grew louder, she leaned back. "Here, listen," she whispered. The moonlight made her smooth skin look almost ethereal. "You can feel it, can't you?"

"Feel what?"

"The blessing."

I closed my eyes and tried to find what she was talking about, but I couldn't feel anything other than the slight chill in the air. "I can't," I said.

"Bummer," she replied.

I agreed. Whatever bliss she was feeling, I wanted a heaping helping.

The song's crescendo faded then it came to an abrupt halt. The six druids within the circle pulled back their hoods, revealing four men and two women. I recognized Simon, with his platinum blond hair, as he strolled to the altar.

He picked up the jug and poured the contents into each of the mortar vessels. He held a glass up as he made eye contact with Luanne. The smile on his face widened. "Let's party," he said. The other druids started laughing, all of them going in for their own cups of the drink, grabbing handfuls of fruits and nuts in the process.

There were two cups left on the altar. Luanne nudged me. "You heard the man. Let's party."

She dragged me into the circle of stones, and I couldn't believe the silence. I mean, I heard the laughing and chatting of the druids, but the sound of crickets and other nature noises disappeared.

"Whoa. This place reminds me of my noise-canceling headphones," I said as I took the offered vessel. There was a dark liquid inside, and I didn't have to be a connoisseur to know the scent of wine. "When in Rome." I tipped the edge of my cup to Lu's, then took a sip. It was sweet with notes of blackberry, orange peel, cinnamon, and a nuttiness I couldn't quite put my finger on. Definitely a dessert wine. "Good."

"It'll get you buzzed," a woman said as she came up to us. Her light brown hair was pulled back into a plaited braid.

"Hellie!" Luanne said. "I didn't realize you were back."

"Simon wanted to surprise you." She kissed Lu on both cheeks.

Simon walked over and put his arm around Hellie. "Surprise."

"You rat." Lu punched Simon in the shoulder. "You should've told me she was coming home." She turned to me. "Hellie, this is my friend Iris. Iris, this is my best friend since my novice days, Hellie Raddison."

"Nice to meet you, Hellie." Her almond-shaped blue eyes made me think she was of Slavic descent. "Interesting name."

"It's a play on Helgade," she said, then laughed when I made a face. "My parents had a thing for old-fashioned names. They named my twin brother Harald."

"Yikes," I said.

Then to my dismay, one of the male druids said, "Everyone calls me Harry." He smiled, putting his dimples on full display.

Lu and Hellie laughed hard then.

"My bad." I held up my hands. "Harald is a fine name."

"I don't mind it," the guy said. "Besides, it was my father's name, and I am proud to have it."

There was a sadness in his tone that I recognized. "I'm sorry."

Harry's expression pinched as he reached out to take Hellie's hand. She didn't reach back, so he let his arm drop back to his side. "Our parents died in a salvo attack during the war."

"Both." My stomach hitched into my chest. I'd lost my mother, and the pain had been unbearable, but to lose both parents at the same time. I couldn't fathom how deep the heartache went. "That's awful."

"War is awful," Hel said quietly.

I knew most of the druids at Iron Grove. At least the ones Lu was friends with were warriors like herself. She'd left the Iron Grove to join the U. S. Army before joining a black ops group until she retired a couple years ago and rejoined her grove as an agent. Did most of the warriors join the military? "Was it Desert Storm?" I asked.

"No," Lu said. "It wasn't a war you would've heard of. It was a ten-year conflict between Iron Grove and Bezoar Grove. We won but at a cost."

"Your grandfather was a great man," one of the male druids said. He had dark hair and dark eyes, giving him a swarthy and mysterious air. "A hero of the war."

Lu's animosity toward Thomas and her grandmother stemmed from her grandfather's death. I wanted to ask a bunch of questions, like why were the two groves at war and how long ago had it been? But there was too much pain in the memory written all over my friend's face.

"Thanks, Finn," Lu said to the dark-hair druid.

"To Kellen Quinn," Simon said.

Everyone raised their glass and drank. Not wanting to offend, I took a swig as well.

"To Harald and Sif," Lu enjoined.

We all drank again. Pretty soon, we were downing drink after drink to the names of fallen heroes until I was so drunk I passed out.

# CHAPTER 5

I RECOGNIZED THE FOREST, BUT HOW? IT WASN'T anything like the cedar and pine that populated the mountain around Southill Village. I blinked, trying to clear my vision and shake the feeling of deja vu.

I'd been here before, right? But I'd never been to Iron Grove before, and since my arrival, I hadn't left the mansion except to follow Luanne through the hedge maze.

The maze, the stone henge, and the altar. And the drinking. God, so much drinking. It's no wonder I was disoriented. Had Lu left me in the maze alone? Had I wandered out into the nearby woods? I shook my head and reached out to brace myself on the trunk of a tree. The bark scraped my palm. The tree coverage allowed very little light from the full moon to filter down, but it was enough to make out a path.

"Follow the trail," I mumbled. I could barely stand, let alone walk. Cripes. I hadn't been this sloshed since New Year's Eve 2003. Evan had booked us a room at a lake resort that had a New Year's package that included an open bar. We'd not only opened the bar, but we'd also closed it. We drank, we danced, we laughed, and in the end, we both puked our guts out after midnight. I'd pretty much sworn off getting blasted since then. Social drinking only. Until tonight. Uck.

On top of being lost in the woods, my bladder was going for the Guinness World Book of Records for how much it could hold before bursting. I was sure these druids didn't keep port-a-potties nearby for emergencies, so my only hope was the house. Where was the house? That freaking thing was so ginormous you could see it from the moon. Yet, no matter which direction I looked, I couldn't see it.

Squishy moss made sucking noises with every step I took. It was the only sound, other than my own breathing that I could hear. That is until I heard a man's voice through the trees.

"*Earth beneath me, sustaining life. Air around me, breathing life. Fire above me, authority of life. Water within me, refreshing life.*" By the end of the incantation, I realized why all this seemed so familiar to me. I'd been here, done that, and got the t-shirt. This was the ritual used when my tera-craft had sparked. It had been a kind of choosing cere-mony. The fade or the bright. Only I hadn't been able to choose. My magic had wanted to take the form of both. As far as I knew, it still did.

The chorus of lovely voices, all in perfect harmony, grew louder and more insistent as I walked the path. And just like the first time, one moment, I was surrounded by dense trees, and the next, I was stepping out into an open field with five tall obelisks arranged in a circle. This wasn't the maze stone henge, but I could see the similarities of purpose. Inside the ring, there were thirteen people in robes and an altar. It was made of four stacked slab stones that were light in color and glowed orange under a blood-red moon.

"Ready the gift," a druid said. He was a tall, thin man with a long scraggly red beard and dark, beady eyes.

I gasped as two men dragged a gagged woman wearing a white shift to the altar. Two more men joined them as she fought to free herself.

"Stop!" I screamed and ran toward them. "Let her go." I gathered my fire, ready to blast them into ash when the woman was free, but they ignored me. And when I called on heat and flame to do my bidding, it ignored me as well. My magic wasn't working. What the fuck?

They tied her down, her dark brown hair a stark contrast to the stone. I tried to help, but my body passed helplessly through the druids, the altar, and the woman. I could smell the woods, the smoke from the burning sage, along with frankincense and lemon grass, but I couldn't touch or interact with anything or anyone in this horrifying scene.

Her wrists and ankles were bound to iron rings at the four corners of the altar. All I could do was watch in horror as the group of bearded monsters circled the desperate young woman.

Red beard stood at the position behind her head. Five bowls were set before him. He took what looked like a smooth tiger eye stone from the first bowl and positioned it at the point where her thighs met her groin.

He circled his hands over the stone, his head tilted to the moon, and said, *"Tera des anu modred caltha wen."*

Next, he scooped liquid from the second bowl and squeezed his fist over her stomach. The woman screamed into her gag, writhing as the droplets wet her.

*"Nero des anu modred caltha wen."*

I sucked back my own scream when he placed a live coal from the third bowl just below her sternum. I turned, running to escape the horror, but no matter where I looked, or I ran, I couldn't get away.

*"Ignis des anu modred caltha wen."*

"Please," I begged. "Stop this." My cry went unanswered.

He blew smoke over her chest. *"Aero des anu modred Caltha wen."*

One by one, the druids held out a hand to Red Beard, and he pierced their palms with the stick, and they squeezed their blood into bowl number five.

Red Beard used the blood to draw a circle with a dot on the scared woman's forehead. *"Anima des anu modred Caltha wen."*

There was a murmur of agreement before the druids joined their voices in an aria to the heavens. Red Beard cupped the woman's cheek. "We thank you for your gifts, *benna-soito.*" And with that, he thrust the white stick into the side of her neck.

*"Aether des anu clofin ahd wen."*

I stumbled back, helpless to do anything, as her eyes widened and light poured from them, dividing by thirteen as each beam moved with purpose into each of the druids. Until they all fell away.

And finally, I was staring at an empty altar. Alone. The moon was no longer bloody, just bright a nearly full.

A woman with bronze skin and dark curly hair hovered above, her dark, golden eyes staring down at me. That's when I realized I was flat on my back. I could hear laughing not that far from where I lay. I reached out, but the woman was just out of my grasp.

"Look with your mind, Iris Everlee, not with your heart. The heart can blind you to what's real."

As she faded away, a sense a peace came over me as fireflies flickered above my body. I smiled. "Hey," I said to my flickering little friends.

"There you are," I heard someone say, and then the night peacefully drifted away.

"TURN OFF THE LIGHTS," I moaned, then rolled over and dragged a pillow onto my head. "It's too early for this much bright."

"It's noon," Keir informed me. "The bright light is called the sun."

I heard the metallic scrape of curtain rings on a rod. Even with my head covered, I could tell the room was darker. Thank heavens. My head was pounding so hard it was as if the Blue Man Group and the entire cast of Stomp were decimating my brain.

"Pain," I whined. "Pain and regret."

"That's what happens when you indulge too much in sacred wine."

I felt a roil of nausea. "Don't say wine." Even hearing

the name of the fermented devil's drink made me ill. I risked a peek from under the pillow. Keir was doing something at the desk. "I think I was poisoned."

"If you mean alcohol poisoning, I think you're probably right."

I threw the pillow at him. "Some sympathy would be nice." I blinked as my sight acclimated to me being alive. I carefully propped myself up on an elbow, trying hard not to jostle my sloshy head. "How did I get back to the room?"

"Lu and Hellie brought you in around two in the morning. You were belting Black Hole Sun by Soundgarden."

"Nooooo," I moaned. I pressed the pillow against my face, praying it would suffocate me on the spot. Black Hole Sun had been my favorite when I was a high school sophomore. Marigold called it my dark phase, and I'll admit, I'd been a melancholic young teen. It made me wonder what the hell had been on my mind at two in the morning that would take me back to my pubescent days.

"You better get up," he said.

"Why?"

"All the archdruids and the coven heads have arrived, and they want to meet with you."

"I thought Freya said we had an extra day."

"Before the testing," Keir agreed. "But not before the talking, apparently."

"Apparently," I muttered. There was nothing inside me that wanted to leave the bed. Nothing. Still, I persevered and overcame, and I managed to sit up. The pounding inside my skull became harder and more insistent. I glanced over at Keir.

He arched a brow. "That bad?"

"Worse," I admitted. "I've drunk some wine in my time, but that stuff kicked my ass."

"The sacramental wine is mixed with blackberry brandy."

I fought my rising gorge as the sacramental wine tried to put in a second appearance. "I did not realize that."

"Yeah, it's the strong stuff too. Like sixty percent alcohol."

I remembered the nightmare the alcohol had given me and shivered. "Never again. I'm pretty sure your sister tried to kill me." I pressed three fingers to my lips as a sourness from my throat hit my mouth. "Oh, God." I jumped up from the bed and ran to the bathroom.

Five minutes later, my stomach was empty. "I hate Lu." Sitting on the bathroom floor, I pressed my face into the cold wall tile. "I can't meet the archdruids and the coven peeps. Not like this."

Keir, who loved me enough to hold my hair out of the toilet for the previous five minutes, washed his hands. He turned to look at me as he dried them on a fluffy green towel. "I'm afraid there's no getting out of it." He raised both brows. "Unless you've changed your mind about running, and if that's the case, I'll go get us packed."

Running sounded like a delightful plan. Not *actual* running, of course. Right now, I was struggling to stay upright. Unfortunately, I wasn't ready to give up my family or my home for the possibility of safety. I grasped the edge of the tub and shoved myself up from the floor to sit on the edge.

Progress.

"I probably should've eaten something." We'd left Freya's without finishing dinner, and I'd ignored the nuts and fruits on the altar. "I'm pretty sure that was straight alcohol coming out of me."

Keir knelt next to me and tucked my hair behind my ear. "I'm sorry you feel bad."

"Do you mean it?" The slight upturn at the corner of his mouth gave me a few doubts.

"When you feel bad, I feel bad."

"Really?"

He smiled and kissed my forehead. "Shower, comb your hair, brush your teeth." He gave me another quick peck. "Not necessarily in that order."

"Har har."

He turned away. "Maybe hit the toothbrush first."

"I'll hit you first."

"Foreplay later." He helped me to my feet. "Archdruids first."

"I hate this," I said as I found my balance. "I feel like I've been tested since I brought the grimoire home. When will it end?"

"Hopefully, in a few days."

"If I'm still alive."

"You'll live," he said with conviction. "You must."

"I hope you found something helpful in those books of yours last night."

"I am not done searching."

"So, nothing." I sighed.

"You're going to need your grimoire," he said. "I called Marigold this morning. She's driving it up here today."

My mood lightened. "Really?"

Keir's smile was soft as he gazed at me. "I hope you don't mind. I thought you might want your sister."

He really did know me. "Thank you, Keir."

"Whatever you need, Iris. I want to give you everything."

"You do," I told him. "Everything and more."

I only wished I could do the same for him.

# CHAPTER 6

HALF AN HOUR LATER AND STILL CURSING THE daylight, I followed Keir to an expansive outdoor dining area. The space was separated from a great room, a room large enough to fit my entire house inside, by a glass pocket door. I tried not to oooo and aaah as the glass disappeared inside the wall.

I don't know what I expected when I'd learned I'd be meeting all the archdruids, but I had a vision of a dozen Gandolf the Grays, Dumbledores, and Merlins gathered around in their gray robes, stroking their gray beards while puffing on long pipes. But no. These four guys and two women looked like they had just ridden their golf carts over from the country club. Freya, however, was sporting Diane Keaton boho-chicness in spades. Her informality was definitely a choice as if to say, *it's my party. I'll casual if I wanna.*

Druid security was posted around the perimeter, and I recognized a few faces, including Lu and Simon, but also the twins, Harry and Hellie, from the night before in the maze. They all had steel gray arm bands adorned with the silhouette of a tree. The druids I didn't recognize wore red, green, purple, brown, yellow, and light blue arm bands with various designs. I assumed they were from the other groves.

Freya made eye contact with me and gave a curt nod. "Good afternoon, Iris. Thank you for joining us."

Like I had a choice. "Afternoon," I replied without a hint of enthusiasm. There was nothing in this world I wanted more right now than to crawl back into bed and sleep until I felt human again. Gratefully, the outdoor patio was covered, and I didn't have to contend with sunlight drilling a hole in my brain. Small favors.

A tall man with dark brown hair and the build of a boxer thrust his hand in my direction. "Ms. Everlee, it is a rare pleasure."

I peered up at him. "Is it? Why?"

"You're somewhat a celebrity in druid and coven circles." He spoke slowly and with a southern accent. "A tru-craft witch with four elements. That's nothing short of a miracle."

I grunted. "Or a curse."

Keir took my hand and gave it a squeeze. A gentle reminder to play nice. My skin warmed, and my concentration sharpened. I laced my fingers in his. The man was better than two aspirins and a good night's sleep.

The brown-haired man, however, was unfazed. He chuckled, then nodded his acquiescence. "Or a curse."

A slight throbbing in my head returned. "Which one are you?" I rubbed my temple with my free hand.

I felt another gentle squeeze, and the throbbing abated. I cast a grateful smile at Keir.

The brown-haired druid gave me a nod. "I'm Derrick Asher, archdruid of the Green Grove."

I recognized the name from our conversation with Freya the night before. "You're the one who suggested the test."

He cocked his head to the side. "Did Freya tell you that?"

I met his gaze. "She did."

"Hmmm." His neatly trimmed brows knitted as he scratched the back of his head. "I see."

I'm glad he did. I was still at a loss. The *malificionito* seemed redundant. I still wasn't sure why they wanted to test my powers. "Why?"

He squinted at me. "Why what?"

A tingle ran along my skin. I pulled my hand from Keir's and rubbed my arms to shake it off. The hangover was really making me feel off. I refocused on Asher. "Why did you want me tested?"

"Because, unlike my peers, I'm not afraid of your growing powers. I see it as a sign for our people." His wide mouth quirked into a smile. "A good omen."

"And the others."

"Some of them agree with me, but a few think you're a danger to our world."

"Spiffy."

"Now, Derrick," a woman said with a New Jersey or New York accent, only not as strong as what I'd heard on television. "Don't monopolize the girl." Her hair was swept up into a clamshell bun with long bangs perfectly framing her face. Her gold and brown hazel eyes raked me with a quick appraisal.

I hadn't been a girl for a very long time, but I'd been taught to respect my elders, so I let it slide. "Hello," I said politely, wondering if she was unaware of how condescending she sounded or if she was just a bitch. "Which one are you?"

"Telva Mack," the woman replied unbothered. "I'm the archdruid of the Luna Grove."

I raised my brow. "You voted against the test." In other words, she had been ready to bind my magic sight unseen. I was putting a mark in the bitch column for her.

"Yes, I did, child. But it matters not." Archdruid Telva spread her hands. "I was out voted."

"Lucky me."

Luna and Bezoar had both voted to bind me. I glanced around, wondering which one of these archdruids was the other asshole. Was it the grumpy guy with the bald head and black goatee? The short woman with curly gray hair, dark skin, and dark brown eyes? The heavy-set dude with the short silver haircut circa 1950? Or lastly, the man with thin blonde hair, a large, hooked nose, and watery blue eyes.

"I think a round of introductions is in order," Freya said, calling everyone's attention. "You all remember Keir," she said, gesturing to my tall drink of druid. "And, as you probably assume, this is Iris Everlee."

"The main attraction," the other woman said. "You're a little long in the tooth for a new tru-crafter."

Since all the archdruids were over seventy, I thought the observation was mildly hypocritical. "I catch on fast."

"So, I've heard." She gave me a sly smile. "I'm Yasmine Leafborne. I am with the Shining River Grove."

Black goatee guy was Jerriah Dale of the Mountain Ash Grove, and the blonde with stringy hair was Mathias Easton of the Bezoar Grove. Not only had the Bezoar archdruid voted against me, but this was the grove that had once been in a war with Iron Grove, resulting in the death of Keir's grandfather. Mathias had moved above Telva to the top of my bitch list.

Harry pushed a cart of donuts, bagels, assorted cream cheeses and jams, and finger sandwiches, along with a coffee pot and a jug of iced tea, toward us. I glanced over to where he'd been standing before with Lu and the others. Damn, I hadn't even noticed he'd left. The sacramental wine had not only kicked my ass, but it had also killed some brain cells.

"Chef Carl sends his regards." Harry gave the archdruids a curt bow. He caught my gaze and winked before departing.

"I see you've met Harry," Keir whispered in my ear.

I smirked. "Barely."

Archdruid Jerriah poured a cup of coffee, and the scent was nirvana.

"I need some caffeine," I told Keir as we sat at the large glass-top table.

"And a donut?" he asked.

"Yes, please." I needed something to replace the electrolytes I lost when I tossed my cookies.

Mathias took the seat to my left. His stringy blond hair fell into his face, and he pushed it back. "Hello." He reminded me of Ichabod Crane from Sleepy Hollow, and not the hot movie or TV version.

"Hey." I clasped my hands together and stared at the table to avoid eye contact. Mathias gave me the creeps. On top of that, he smelled faintly of boiled cabbage.

He scratched the bridge of his large nose. "It's quite chilly this afternoon."

It was seventy-two degrees out. For late September in Northern Wisconsin, it was unseasonably warm. I shrugged. "Could be worse."

Keir set a small plate and a steaming mug in front of me, then took the seat to my right. "Everything okay."

"Peachy keen." I forced a tight smile. "Just talking about the weather with Archdruid Mathias."

"Sounds scintillating," Derrick said as he took the chair across from us. "Mathias has always been such a sparkling conversationalist."

Mathias sneered at the Green Grove's archdruid. "Ever the smart ass."

"Now, Matty, don't be surly."

Derrick's tone was one of jest, but Matty looked unamused. Good. Maybe if the Green Grove archdruid made the Ichabod look-alike uncomfortable enough, he'd move away from me. I covered my amusement by taking a sip of coffee and a bite of the cinnamon twist Keir had brought me. A moan of bliss escaped me as I chewed the sweet, spicy, pillowy goodness of fried dough.

A tinkling of glass put an end to the familiar banter. Freya tapped her spoon against her orange juice glass a few more times and then said, "Now that we're all settled in, let's get down to business."

I nudged Keir with my elbow and spoke to him out the side of my mouth. "Sounds good to me." Now that I'd had some caffeine and carbs, the hangover started to lift. I noticed a distinct lack of other druids, but I remembered Freya saying the heads of the covens were coming for the testing as well. "Where are the witches?"

Telva sat down next to Derrick.

Awesome. Not.

"The tru-craft coven leaders will be arriving tonight," Telva gave me an interested look that made me wish she was less interested. "They're eager to meet the wonder kid."

"Cool, cool," I said quickly and took another bite of my donut twist, barely tasting it this time.

Truth was, I wanted to meet other tru-craft witches. The last few months, I'd been supported by my family, my new friends, and Keir. Even so, in some ways, I'd felt very alone. Especially when it came to my magic. I needed other people who knew what I was going through in my life. That's why I'd shared so much with Thomas. He'd been the first of my kind that I'd ever spoken with. He'd made me feel safe and understood. Mostly because he understood.

I wagged the floppy confection of deliciousness at Telva. "I look forward to meeting them."

Her response sounded deliberate and calculated as her eyelids lowered in a spectacularly dramatic fashion. "As I'm sure they're looking forward to meeting you, Iris."

That wasn't ominous at all. "Awesome possum," I said before I could stop myself. I was a competent woman with an advanced degree in English, but I sounded like I'd traveled back in time to high school Iris. I groaned inwardly and wished I had a time machine that could dial back my words to a few seconds earlier. "I mean, yay." There. So much better.

"Now that you've had a chance to meet Iris, I wonder if the *malificionito* is even necessary," Freya said. Even though I knew it was pie-in-the-sky wishing, I appreciated her trying. "She doesn't pose a danger to our kind or hers. I don't think we can blame her for the events surrounding the initiation of her gifts."

"Yes, yes, Freya. We all know where you stand on the subject. You made your objections perfectly clear," Jerriah of Mountain Grove stated. He stroked the end of his black goatee. "You have been heard and overruled. Ms. Everlee will be tried and tested, or she will be silenced."

Alarm and the urge to run rushed through me. "Silenced?"

"You're magic," Derrick explained.

"Oh, yeah, right." Silenced in the movies and books usually ended with someone's throat cut. Although, if I didn't survive the testing, the outcome would be much the same.

Keir slammed his hand onto the table. "This isn't a traditional *malificionito*. Iris is indisputably a tru-craft witch."

"You're point?" Matthias asked. He sounded bored, but I could see a spark of interest in the slight arch of his brow.

I took that as my cue to show the archdruids what I was made of, so I summoned fire from my blood to light a three-wick candle on the table. Unfortunately, my pulse kicked up a notch and the tingling from earlier buzzed along my arms and up the back of my neck, causing a power spike. The candle shot fire from its wicks like a triple-shot flame thrower. I grimaced. "Ta-dah," I said weakly.

Cripes. If I made it through this week alive and with my magic intact, I'd never drink ritual wine again.

The throbbing in my head spiked, the pain sharp and breathtaking.

"Are you okay?" Keir asked.

"My brain feels like it's going to explode," I gritted out through clenched teeth. My eyes began to water, clouding my vision.

Keir grasped my shoulders and turned me toward him. "Your eyes are bleeding."

I scrambled to my feet, but they felt clumsy and wooden, air lifted my hair from my shoulders, and my veins burned. "What's happening to me?"

"It's magic," Derrick said with urgency. "Take her somewhere isolated before this gets worse."

Before I could protest, Keir swept me from my feet and carried me away.

# CHAPTER 7

Sweat soaked my back. My neck refused to support the weight of my head, and it bounced around as Keir ran down the halls with me.

"Hold on," he said. "I have you. Just stay with me."

His voice had deepened to an unrecognizable tone. His puca tended to rear its ugly head whenever I was in danger.

The boiling heat inside me grew with every one of his footfalls.

"Here," I heard someone say. "Bring her inside."

I tried to look toward the voice, but my eyeballs were on fire, and everything looked blurry through the flames. My arms were limp at my sides as a sudden chill swept over me, and the fire turned to ice. Shit. I'd only felt this way once before, and I'd ended up in the hospital because my earth magic had been destroying me at a cellular level. I couldn't keep one prevailing thought from my head: this is dying. I am dying.

"You're not dying," I heard Keir growl.

Had he heard my thoughts? No. I had to have said it aloud, but I'm not sure how. I could barely get my brain to work, let alone my mouth.

"Lay her down on the bed," the voice in charge said. It was a man, but that's all I could work out.

Keir cradled me tighter. "No," he told the guy. "I'm not letting her go."

I expected a protest. None came. "Fine," the man said. "But you're extremely tall right now. I'll need you to sit down with her so I can perform my examination."

He was a doctor or maybe a medic. I hadn't realized Iron Grove had a clinic on-site, but it made sense. A lot of training went on at the mega-mansion. Someone was bound to pull a groin.

As Keir sat down, my backside on his lap, I wanted to reassure him that I'd be all right, but my words came out like a garbled groan.

"What's wrong with her?" Keir asked.

It was the question of the hour.

I began to shiver as ice water traveled through my veins. "Ssss-ss-ssss," was all that I could manage of the phrase, so cold. Why was this happening? Other than a hangover, I'd been fine moments before...

...Until I'd called on fire. I'd used my ignis-craft to light the candles then I'd felt as if the fire had gone wild inside me. Was my magic betraying me again? Of course, it was. Had being around all those archdruids somehow amplified my powers? Maybe.

Cripes. If that was the case, even if I managed to survive now, what chance did I stand at surviving the tests?

"She's spiked a fever," the man said. "It's eating at her craft."

"Do something," Keir told him. "Fix her."

Tears leaked from my eyes, burning as they trailed down my temples to my ears. I hadn't said goodbye to my family. Michael was almost an adult, but he still needed me. This wasn't the end. I'd beat turning to dust before, and I could do it again. I was made of minerals, fire, air, and water, and I had the power to control at least three of those things.

I sipped the air, my lungs hot from the wild magic coursing through me, and I mentally reached for a thread to pull that would unravel the mysteries inside me. I searched my muscles, bones, blood, and, finally...just there, like an ant crawling around under my skin, I found something that shouldn't be.

I moaned as I plucked at the elusive thing, constantly moving.

"Why is she writhing?" Keir asked. "Is she having as seizure?"

I felt cool hands on my cheeks. "I don't think so," the man said. "She's trying to fight whatever's happening to her."

"Can you stop it?"

There was a pause, and I could almost feel the unsaid no. "I can try to combine my magic with hers, but since I don't know what she's doing or how she's fighting it, I'm afraid I could make the situation worse."

I chased the ant as it traversed my stomach and up my chest. When it hit my throat, I was sure I'd trapped it. The feel of the damn thing was so foreign, like nothing I'd ever felt. Could it be my nero-craft trying to rear its watery head? Maybe. But it didn't feel like it belonged.

A sharp pain in my jaw made me jerk and stretch my body and neck straight. I bit down a scream as I chased the ant up my cheek. I wanted it out, and if I couldn't pluck the son-of-a-bitch, I would burn it out. I called on my fire, sending it through capillaries and veins like heat-seeking missiles on a mission.

"Her face is flushed, and her skin is getting hotter," the man said. "She's going to burn up if we don't get her iced. We have to cool her down."

"No," Keir said in a way that brooked no argument. "Whatever has a hold on her, she's fighting it, and she's winning."

Was I? He sounded more confident than I felt, but as the fire burned under my skin, I knew the moment the foreign ant was trapped. Unfortunately, it was right between my eyes.

Bone cages, Fire purges, Air expels, I thought. The bones in my forehead created a ridged barrier as fiery blood filled the spot, and the air in my blood tried to shove it out of my skin. I could feel the ant scurrying, looking for a way to escape the prison I'd made, but I'd set the trap too well. Bone cages, fire purges, air expels, I thought again and again until I felt my lips moving to the incantation.

"What's that on her forehead?" the man asked.

"It's a circle," Keir said.

"Is she doing that?"

I was. I had the rogue entity trapped, but I could feel

my body weakening and, with it, my magic. I couldn't let go. Not now. Not when I was so close.

"She's getting weaker," Keir said. "I can feel it. Help her."

"I've never seen anything like this. I wish I knew how." The man sounded as desperately dejected as Keir. "Your soul bond with her is the only thing keeping her in this battle," he added. "I pray it's enough."

I felt a warmth on my stomach. Not the heat or fire of my blood, but something else. Then the warmth began to vibrate.

"Bob," I rasped out.

I could hear the smile on Keir's lips. "He's here, Iris," he said. "Bob and I are both here. We're here for you."

It was the extra-energy I needed. Air expels. I put all my intent into the words and said them out loud. "Air expels."

"Air expels," the man repeated.

"Air expels," we said together.

A knot formed in the circle, like a massive zit.

"Air expels," the man said again.

The zit popped. The ant was gone, and the fire inside me receded.

"What the hell?" Luanne asked. "What is that?" I hadn't realized she was in the room, but it was unsurprising she'd shown up to check on me.

"Something not of Iris's making," the man informed her. "Someone tried to spell her with anima."

"Is she safe?" Keir asked.

"For now," the man said.

"Then get out," Keir told him. "All of you."

All of them? How big of an audience had I attracted? Did I really want to know?

Once the door closed, Keir pulled me close to his chest, and Bob got out of the way. "You have to quit scaring me like that. I don't know what I'd do without you."

Surprising myself, I managed to string words together to make a sentence. "I'm not planning on going anywhere," I replied. "Wherever you go, that's where I'll be."

"That's a lovely sentiment." He brushed his lips across mine. "How are you feeling?"

"Better," I told him.

"Can you sit up?"

I wiggled my toes and flexed my fingers, relieved that I could move them at will.

"I think so."

Slowly, Keir sat me up on his lap, his arm circling my waist to steady me. "Thanks." I shook my head. "I don't know what happened. I mean, I been feeling like crap since I got up, but that was like all my magic decided to jump my ass all at once." I wiped the wetness on my cheeks. "Am I still bleeding?"

"Nothing fresh, except for a small amount oozing from your forehead."

"From the magical zit," I said.

He tucked his chin and then coughed on a laugh. "A magical what?" The inky blackness in his eyes had been replaced by his normally gorgeous gray. The danger was gone for the moment, and with it, his puca had gone dormant.

"A magical zit that needed popping," I cradled his cheek and kissed him back. "Do you have your phone on you?"

"Yes," he said. "Why?"

"Because I want to see what kind of mess I made of my face."

Keir shifted beneath me and then pulled up his phone. He unlocked it with his fingerprint and then handed it to me. I pulled up the camera, turned the lens to me and stifled a gasp. There were streaks of dried blood crusting under my eyes and down my cheeks, but my gaze went directly to my forehead.

"I've seen that before." I examined the bloody circle where my bone and blood had cut through my skin, along with the eruption in the middle.

Keir narrowed his gaze on me. "It's the alchemy symbol for spirit."

"That's why the doctor said I'd been spelled with anima." When Keir first told me about the five types of elemental magic, he'd mention spirit or anima-craft as the fifth element. "Anima-craft is spirit magic, right? The same kind of magic Bogmall had used to possess Yolanda, the cheer mom."

I remember Keir had also warned me that spirit magic drew its power from the very soul of the world. The magic involved channeling and summoning spirits to fuel spellwork. And, he'd said, it was the most dangerous of the five. It was why anima-craft witches were so uncommon. A novice witch rarely survived the spark. Which meant, Bogmall had managed to either find a novice before he or she died, or she had defeated a truly powerful tru-crafter to become the Hexen-bitch she was today.

"Where did you see the symbol?" Keir asked. "Was it in a book? Did Bogmall use it? Or did you see it more recently, like here at Iron Grove?"

"More recent," I said. "I had a dream last night." I met his gaze. "At least I thought it was only a dream." I shivered, remembering the woman strapped down and gagged on the altar. "Men in robes performed a ritual, and they drew this symbol on a woman's forehead. Their leader, a red-bearded guy, used blood from all the other robed guys to trace it. He said something like anima call to wind. Then thanked her for her gifts right before he killed her with a white stick and mainlined her energy as it streamed from her eyes."

"Why didn't you tell me?" His voice held an edge.

"I was hungover and being rushed to brunch," I said a little defensively. "Besides, it hadn't felt real. Even now, thinking back on it, it feels like a dream. I couldn't do anything to help the woman. I was an invisible observer."

"I'm sorry. I'm worried, is all." He took my hand in his and gave me a reassuring squeeze. "Have you seen any of these men at Iron Grove?"

I shook my head. "They all looked...out of time. You know, as if plucked from ancient history. Long beards, craggy faces, and it was all men other than the sacrifice." I got up from Keir's lap. Bob began to weave his body around and between my legs, his purring growing loud. I reached down and picked him up, welcoming the calm that holding him brought me. "You don't think it's ancient history, do you?"

"Not as ancient as I'd like," Keir said. "Not nearly."

"The doctor said an anima spell was put on me. Do you think it might have happened when I passed out in the maze last night?"

"Maybe." Keir rubbed his temples and then stood up. "I'm sorry, Iris. If I had known how dangerous coming to the Iron Grove would be for you, I'd have never brought you."

"It was my decision, and I'm here. No going back. Only forward. Besides, am I safe anywhere? That hasn't been true since the first time I sparked to tru-craft." If I'd learned anything from the past few months, it was that danger was everywhere. "Maybe the doctor might know more about the magic used on me."

Keir gave me a crooked smile. "It wasn't a doctor."

"Medic, nurse, doctor, whatever. The guy seemed like he might know something."

My long-legged druid strode across the room and opened the door. "She wants to talk to Thomas," he said.

"Thomas?" My heart jumped in my chest as a thin man, shorter than I imagined, but with the same kind face and crazy hair, I'd seen on my laptop screen so many times. A smile spread on my lips, and my eyes widened as the man gave me a gentle nod. "Thomas!" I set Bob on the bed and then crossed the room to the older tru-craft witch. I held out both my hands, and he took them. "I'm so happy to finally meet you."

"Hello, Iris Everlee." He smiled back at me, but I could see the worry in his crinkled eyes. "I wish our meeting was under better circumstances."

"If wishes were horses." It was something my mother

used to say whenever any of my siblings would use the word wish.

"Then beggars would ride," Thomas finished.

Mom had explained that the saying meant people shouldn't waste time on wishing because if wishes were real, then no one would ever be sick or poor. She called it magical thinking. Little did she know, magic was real. Even so, she hadn't been wrong about wishing. It never helped anyone. The only way a person could make any real change was by doing what needed to be done.

"Tell me how someone would have put a spell on me," I said, "and teach me how to prevent it from happening again."

"It's not that easy. It takes weeks of practice to create effective blocks against invasive spells."

I grasped his hands firmly and met his wizened gaze. "We have one day."

He nodded. "Then we better get to it."

# CHAPTER 8

As soon as I could, I washed the dried blood, which made me look as if I had Ebola, from my face. I leaned in close to the mirror, glad that the circle of bone had receded and started to heal. The idea of walking around with a bullseye on my forehead seemed a little too on the money for my life. Even so, while the big circle was completely gone, the small eruption in the center was slow to go.

"Why won't the damn hole in my forehead close?" Thomas had tried a healing incantation in the medic room, using some marshmallow bark. It had helped a little, but I still looked as if I had a giant, angry zit for a third eye.

"I feel like I'm fifteen-years-old again, and it's the night of prom," I complained.

"Sounds traumatic," Lu said in a bored, slightly sarcastic way. The druid warrior had escorted Keir, Thomas, and me to Thomas's quarters on the west side of the mega-mansion.

I rolled my eyes at her reflection in the mirror. "If you're not going to be helpful, you can go."

"Sorry," she replied. "I must've left my magical acne cream in my other purse."

I snickered at the visual. Luanne never carried a purse. Hell, I'd rarely seen her in anything other than black. She was the only person I knew who could wear black from head to toe, though, and not look like she was trying to be goth. On the contrary, Luanne always looked like a bad ass soldier of fortune. No one picked a fight with Lu. At least not more than once.

I turned around and leaned my butt against the vanity. "What am I going to do?"

"It'll heal," Lu said bluntly. "You've had way worse injuries."

There was a dry washcloth neatly folded near the faucet. I chucked it at Lu. "I'm not talking about my forehead. I mean about the testing."

"You'll kick the crap out of it." Lu shrugged with nonchalance. "You always do."

"I appreciate the vote of confidence, but there's no way I accidentally got spelled. Someone is working against me, and they nearly succeeded today."

There was a hard edge to the lines around her eyes as she pinched the bridge of her nose for a moment and then put her hand on my shoulder. "We'll find out who did this, Iris. I swear it. They won't get near you again."

"The problem is I don't remember them getting near me the first time. It had to be when I passed out in the maze. Do you remember me leaving the henge area? I can kind of remember some fireflies flitting around above me, and then I had the sacrifice dream."

"Are you sure it was a dream? Not another between walk, like when you met our druid circle when your tera-craft sparked?"

I'd woken up in the middle of the night in the woods, much like I had in the dream the night before, but when I'd done the between walk, I was a participant at the altar. I shook my head. "It was vivid enough, but I was like a ghost. A mere witness to a really awful scenario."

"A scenario that happened way too often in the past," Thomas said at the door.

I smiled at the wizened older man. "And the not-so-past." Earlier, I'd described the dream in full to all three of them.

He nodded his agreement. "But no longer sanctioned," he amended. "From what you described, you witnessed an Awakening ritual. It was a way to share life and power in a druid circle. A symbiosis between our kind and theirs."

"Only this wasn't symbiotic," I told him. I couldn't keep the anger out of my tone. "That woman wasn't *sharing* anything with those men. She was being robbed of her magic and her life."

"That's not how it was supposed to work, but all too often, it did. Some people want power to help make the world around them a better place, some want safety, some want status, and some want more power. Every type can justify some extremely horrific acts because they believe they have a good reason. That their wants entitle them." He scratched a bushy brow. "Even so, there aren't any druids at Iron Grove who look the way you described."

"Yeah, I haven't seen anyone with a long scraggly beard around here," I agreed. "It's why I thought it was a dream." I glanced over at Lu. She had jammed her hands in her pockets and was staring at the ground. "You okay?"

She grunted an affirmative, then said, "I'll wait for you out there." On that note, she brushed past Thomas without a single acknowledgment and left the bathroom.

I made eye contact with Thomas. "She has a giant bug up her butt about you."

He gave me a half smile that didn't reach his eyes. "That's one way of putting it."

"She blames you for her grandfather's death."

Thomas winced.

My words were blunter than I'd intended. "I'm sorry. I shouldn't have—"

He held up his hands. "It's fine. You're not wrong."

"Are you responsible?"

"No. That part is wrong. But Luanne does blame me. Maybe more than Freya." He rubbed his eyes with his thumb and forefinger. "It's a story for another time. How are you feeling?"

"Better." My body aches and pains from earlier were almost completely gone. Even the hangover headache had disappeared. The only part of me that really hurt was the hole in my forehead. "How can I stop this from happening again? You said there were ways to protect myself."

"There are." He splayed his hands wide. "It's not an easy fix."

"What else is new?" Tru-craft had been a lot of things since I'd first sparked to it. Easy wasn't one of them.

"What do I need to do?"

Thomas tugged at the hem of his sweater and then lifted it up to his chest. On his stomach was a colorful, heavily lined tattoo of a forest green circle inside a golden yellow circle, some symbols in black in between the gap that I didn't recognize, and a fancy knotted triangle at the center of the green circle with lines of indigo blue, black, and red. The artwork covered the entirety of his abs.

I let out a low whistle. "Son of a bitch. That looks like it was painful."

"You have no idea." He let go of his sweater. "It's a protection sigil. The center has a triquetra. It's used to confuse any magic that gets past the initial wards. Keeps the foreign spell busy until it runs its course."

"How long did you sit for that tattoo?"

"An hour a day for three weeks."

"Twenty-one hours?" I let out another low whistle. "On the stomach. Yikes."

"I was a much younger man. I'm not sure I could sit through it again."

"That bad?"

"Worse." He snorted a short laugh. "The pigments used in the sigil are derived from plants like sunflowers, yarrow, indigo, madder, and tansy combined with other protection herbs. The burning was intense."

"Well, that sounds terrible."

"Then I'm describing it correctly." He sighed. "Even if I could gather all the pigments, I'm not sure the eclectic witch who performed the ritual is available on short notice."

"Eclectic witch?"

"They practice a combination of crafts instead of just one."

"Are they born witches like me?"

"Not usually, but in my friend's case, yes. He was born tera-craft but never sparked." Thomas shrugged. "It happens."

This wasn't news to me. Even though Michael had been born tru-craft, he might never develop powers. It was rarer in the male born.

"So, that's a big fat no to getting a tattoo before the witch trials."

Thomas chuckled. "We will figure something out."

For the first time since I'd expelled the magic zit, I took stock of the fact that I was standing in front of Thomas, a man who had, for the past few weeks, acted as a mentor and a friend. Even now, he was doing everything in his power to help me. Impulsively, I crossed the bathroom and gave him a hug.

After only the briefest of pauses, he hugged me back.

"Thank you," I told him before letting him go.

"For what?"

"For being super cool."

"Baby, I was born that way."

I grinned. "A Gaga reference?"

"Who else?" He smirked. "Come on. You have visitors."

"I do?"

He backed out of the bathroom. I followed him down the hall. I heard a familiar voice in the living room and quickened my pace.

Marigold, Luanne, and Keir were huddled together,

having a chat, in the middle of the room. My sister wore her dark hair up in a loose bun. She had a jade hair pin sticking from the top, holding the masterpiece in messy chic in place. Her brown eyes landed on me as I burst from the hall.

"Marigold!"

"Iris!" She hugged me hard. "It feels like you've been gone for weeks."

"Same," I told her. "I'm so glad you're here." We let go of each other. "Things are getting pretty intense around here."

Luanne snorted. "Master of the understatement."

"Intense is a pretty good description," Keir said in my defense.

Marigold leaned back as she peered at my face. She poked a finger at my forehead. "What happened there? You didn't shoot yourself with a BB gun, did you?"

When I was twelve, Marigold had stolen a BB gun from a boy she liked, and the two of us had made a day of trying to shoot every offending leaf and twig we could hit. Our younger sister Rose happened upon us and threatened to tell Mom. Now, I'd discovered on my afternoon adventures that I had a better chance of hitting the lottery than the broadside of a barn. Even so, when I haphazardly took aim at my sister and shot the air-driven weapon, a BB hit smack dab in the middle of her forehead and stuck. When she flicked it out, the wound it left behind looked a lot like the wound the foul spirit spell had created after I'd expelled it from my skin.

Before I could answer Marigold's question, though, Lu said, "Somebody spelled her with magic and tried to fry her with her own abilities. Iris spit it right out her forehead."

"I didn't spit it."

The warrior druid shrugged.

Marigold's eyes widened with alarm. "So, how do we stop it from happening again?"

The corner of my mouth quirked up into a half-grin. I loved how Marigold said "we." "Unfortunately, the process takes longer than I have."

"What process?" Keir asked.

"It's a protection tattoo about the size of a dinner plate," I oversimplified. "Thomas has one on his stomach. It took twenty-one hours to complete, and that's with someone who had the right ingredients."

Keir narrowed his gaze at Thomas. "Can I see?"

Luanne rolled her eyes and sucked her teeth.

Keir gave her a scolding gaze.

She dropped her arms to her sides and shook her head. She rolled her hand at Thomas. "Let's see it."

I didn't love the rudeness from either of them toward Thomas, but I didn't share their history with the man.

Thomas, unperturbed by either of them, lifted his shirt.

Marigold let out a low whistle.

I laughed, and all four of them looked at me.

"I had the same reaction," I explained. It was yet more proof that blood didn't make a family. Marigold and I might have had different biological parents, but our habits, things we said, certain mannerisms that we shared exposed us as family all the same.

Keir had leaned over for a closer look at the tattoo.

"There's Icelandic symbols, some Norse, Celtic, modern Wicca, and even demonic. Who drew the sigils?" His tone was a mixture of impressed with a hint of disapproval.

"A friend," Thomas said.

"An eclectic witch," I filled in. The old witch could defend himself, but I felt the urge to protect him. "A trucraft born witch who never sparked."

"Ah." Keir nodded; his lips pursed. "That makes more sense." He sighed. "Obviously, this isn't an option."

"No. Even if my friend was available, it would take too long, and Iris wouldn't recover enough for *malificionito*."

"Is your friend available?" Marigold asked.

"I'm not getting a tattoo," I told her.

Marigold ignored me. "Is he?" she asked Thomas again.

"I don't know," he replied. "Why?"

Marigold reached around behind her head and used the bun pick to scratch her scalp. "It might be dumb."

I gave my sister a nudge. "Tell us what you're thinking."

She stared at Thomas's tattoo. "Does the symbol have to be inked into the skin?"

He arched a brow at her.

"I work the henna booth at Southill Village Fair every year. If your friend has the supplies and the drawing, I could paint it onto Iris's skin. It wouldn't take that long. As long as she doesn't wash it off, it should last for a couple of days. I can reapply as she needs it." I think we were all gaping because Marigold added, "It's stupid, right?"

"A temporary tattoo." Thomas shook his head and let his shirt drop. "My dear, you are a genius."

I tamped down a surge of hope. "Will it work?"

"I'll call my friend and find out," Thomas said. "Give me a couple of minutes." He sped from the living room and down the narrow hall.

I hugged Marigold again before stepping back to meet her gaze. "How did I get so lucky?"

She winked at me. "Just blessed, I guess."

"If this works," Lu said. "I'm buying drinks."

Marigold lightly jabbed her with an elbow. "Cynic."

"Realist," Lu countered.

I laughed. Having my sister here really had been the best medicine. I felt lighter than I'd felt since coming to Iron Grove.

Keir smiled at me. "Your head wound is closing."

"Is it?" I touched the spot. It felt like a tiny bump now. "That's good news."

As I let my hand drop, a rock from out of nowhere smacked me in the forehead. "Ouch." The pebble had hit dead center on the magical zit. "That really fucking hurt."

"Stupid, *Klienkind*." The crisp German-accented speech surprised and elated me. "When will you learn to duck?"

"Linda." Marigold gave the gnome a cross look. "Unless you want to walk home, stop throwing stuff at Iris."

"Walking would be safer," Linda muttered.

I didn't care about getting pelted with rocks—I mean, I did care—but if the result was having Linda or not having Linda, I would take the headaches. "I can't believe you came. And in a car."

The gnome's cheeks turned as pink as her outfit. "Where else would I be?"

A rhythmic tapping on the glass pane drew our attention. Outside, his wings buzzing so fast they were a colorful blur, was Fair Konig, king of the Southill Village pixies. "I am here, Iris Everlee, ready to fulfill my debt to you and your kin."

Marigold winced. "Oh, yeah, the pixie insisted on coming as well."

Keir walked over, opened the window, and slid up the screen to let Fair Konig inside.

My brows raised as I gave my sister a pitying glance. "That must've been a fun car ride."

She groaned. "You have no idea."

Thomas walked back into the living room, barely registering surprise. "My friend will be here between seven and eight tonight."

"Does he think it can be done?" Keir asked.

Thomas spread his hands before him. "He doesn't know, but he's willing to try."

# CHAPTER 9

I waited out on the balcony of Thomas' modest quarters. The view overlooked the hedge maze. I tried to recall the night from the time I took my first sip of wine until I woke up in the room I shared with Keir. Other than the horrific dream, the night was a blank.

Luanne joined me. "The tattoo dude is here."

"Hey." I touched her arm before she could go back inside. "What happened?"

"When?"

"At the party last night. I can't remember anything after the first couple of goblets of wine."

The druid warrior gave me a curious look. "Really?"

"Nope. I mean, I kind of remember lying on the ground and playing with some fireflies, but everything else was blank until I woke up today. Keir said the sacramental stuff you guys drink is strong, but I've drank moonshine that didn't put me on my ass like this."

"Do you think you were drugged?"

"Maybe." When I first sparked to magic, I was certain

I'd been drugged. I'd been wrong, but it had seemed like a logical conclusion. Logical didn't make it right. "Do you think the wine..."

Lu shook her head and waved her hand to dismiss the idea. "We all drank from the same jug. We would've all been drugged."

"What about the cup? Could someone have laced it with something before giving it to me?"

Her forehead creased as she frowned. "Simon poured the glasses of wine and dished them out. If one of them was drugged, he wouldn't have known to give it to you."

"What if Simon drugged me?"

Lu's gaze sharpened. "I trust him with my life."

"How about my life?"

Some of the simmering anger dissipated. "Yes. With your life too. Simon is loyal to a fault. He wouldn't do it."

I shrugged, putting aside my doubts. If Luanne had that much faith in the white-haired druid, then I had to believe she knew what she was talking about. Unless... "I was hit with spirit magic."

"That's what Thomas says."

"What if this is Bogmall again? She possessed Yolanda to get to me. Could she take over someone like Simon?"

Lu's denial was emphatic. "No." She shook her head and gave a slight shrug of doubt. "Maybe." She chewed the side of her thumbnail. "I don't know, honestly. I hope I'd be able to tell, but Bogmall used to be one of our leaders. She and Simon were close for a period of time. She would know him well enough to fake being him...at least for a little while."

My stomach dipped as the pit in my gut grew more

cavernous. I didn't know exactly how spirit magic worked. Could Bogmall enter anyone? Was her reach unlimited? The idea of her somehow infiltrating Iron Grove without anyone noticing scared the crap out of me. Would she jump into someone intimately close to me? Lu? Keir? My sister? I blew out a noisy sigh. "How can I trust anyone when my worst enemy can inhabit people I love the most?"

"Ask me something only I would know," Lu challenged.

"How did you introduce yourself to me when we first met?" I asked.

"I told you that I took your class my freshman year at Darling University."

I nodded. "You're good."

"Unless Bogmall knew what cover I was going to use...." She gave me a sly smile.

"It's you," I said blandly, then added, "Smart ass."

She looped her arm across my shoulders. "Come on. It's time to see the wizard."

"If I tapped my heels together three times, do you think they'd let me go home?"

Lu snorted. "That's a whole different book, Dorothy."

"I'd be okay with a house falling on a certain sorceress."

"The minute a monkey sprouts wings and takes to the skies, you're on your own."

"You'd desert me?"

"Never," she replied. "Now, no more stalling."

"Fine." I nodded toward the French doors. "Lead the way."

I lifted my head and pulled my shoulders back, affecting confidence I didn't feel, as we walked back into the apartment.

Marigold was sitting on a large comfy chair with Bob curled up in her lap. Keir and Thomas were talking with a man who stood at Keir's height, who I assumed was Thomas's friend. He was younger than I'd imagined. He looked to be in his late thirties or early forties. I'd thought he'd be closer to Thomas' age, not mine.

"Iris." Thomas waved me over. "Come meet Carver."

The man extended a bone-thin hand. I took it. His cuticles were stained in various colors. He worked with pigments and inks, so a hazard of the job, I supposed.

He studied my face for a beat, then said, "I hear you need a protection sigil," he said genially. He had unusually high cheekbones, a wide mouth, and a hawk-like nose. His light brown hair was disheveled and a bit messy.

"I need something," I agreed. I let go of his hand and glanced at Keir for reassurance. He positioned himself next to me, the back of his hand brushing against mine. Just that barest touch bolstered my spine.

Carver held a leather-bound case in his left hand. It was covered in glyphs and alchemy symbols. I recognized a few of them from one of Keir's many books. Did I know what they meant? Absolutely not. I made a mental note to double down on my magical studies if I lived through the week. "What's in the box?" I asked.

"My kit." Carver set the case onto the breakfast bar separating Thomas' kitchen from his living room. I moved in for a closer look. The locking mechanism was a Cryptex with at least two dozen cipher dials.

"Elaborate," Luanne said. "But not foolproof." She touched the lock. "I could get through it."

The corners of Carver's lips tugged into an amused smile. "Go for it," he said.

Lu eagerly rubbed her fingertips together. "Piece of cake," she mused. Holding the Cryptex between her two hands, she pulled on the right side while simultaneously pushing the dials toward the right with her left hand.

"What are you doing?"

"There is a ridge inside each dial that, when lined up with the arrows," she pointed to the two arrows on either side of the device, "will allow the center to slide out, and the lock will be opened. By pushing the dials to the right, turning becomes a little more difficult until the bumps catch on the groove...." She grinned as she stopped turning the first dial. "Just like that. Only twenty-three to go."

Carver looked non-plussed as he watched Luanne have eureka moments as she moved through each section until the very last. She stared at the jumble of letters and symbols across the dials and shook her head. "Of course, it's nonsense. Harder to crack that way. Luckily, my way doesn't require logic."

The thin man gestured to the case. "To the victor goes the spoils."

Lu looked over her shoulder and winked at me. "Voila." She pulled on the right side and then frowned. "Voila," she said again and gave it a more insistent tug. Again, nothing happened. "I know I got the Cryptex right," she told Carver. "Why isn't it opening?"

"Because not all puzzles are created equal," the

eclectic witch told her. He took a stylus from his pocket and pricked his thumb. He wiped his blood across the Cryptex and muttered an incantation. The right side slid free of the left.

"You added a spell element." Lu sounded impressed. "I should've realized."

"Yes, warrior," Carver agreed with a smirk. He opened the case, and it unfolded like a tackle box with extra shelves that raised up on hinges. One side was full of small apothecary bottles with a variety of cork, wood, and metal stoppers. The other side was full of small plastic resealable baggies that were full of colorful powders. The top shelves had instruments that looked to be made of bleached bones with sharply pointed iron nails on the ends.

"That looks like a torture kit," I said.

"It's going to be a long night. We should begin."

My eyes felt like saucers as he withdrew one of the tools that had a nail on the end. "Aren't you just going to lick and stick?"

Carver frowned. "Excuse me."

I gave Thomas a pointed look. "You did tell him that I just wanted the tattoo drawn on me, right? No skin poking required."

The eclectic witch arched a brow at Thomas. "I told you that wouldn't work."

"I should've known." Luanne scoffed and angrily huffed. "You can't trust Darrencroft," she said. "He's a snake."

I wanted to defend Thomas, but I couldn't stop

thinking about those pointy nails hammering into my skin.

The old tru-crafter managed to appear chagrined. "You're one of the most talented practitioners of protection spells that I know," he said in his defense. "And Iris needs protection."

"But not in the form of a twenty-hour tattoo," I added.

"It won't work." Carver scratched his nose. "The pigments I derive from herbs and minerals have different staining times. If even one-line rubs away, blurs or dissolves, the sigil is rendered useless."

"Well, that sucks."

"I'm sorry, Iris," Marigold said. "I thought I'd really solved it."

I grabbed her hand and gave it a squeeze. "It was a good idea."

"Good idea's work," she replied.

I sighed and leaned against the counter. "Bogmall wins again."

Keir's voice was sharp with alarm. "Bogmall? Do you think she's responsible for the spirit spell?"

"I don't know." I reached into Carver's case and touched one of the nail barbs. It felt icy and hot at the same time. I jerked my hand back. "Lu and I were bouncing the idea around. She possessed a cheerleader's mom. What's to stop her from possessing someone here at Iron Grove?"

Carver narrowed his gaze at me and steepled his fingers. "Please, elaborate. How did Bogmall possess a cheerleader?"

"Cheerleader's mom," Marigold corrected, then shook her head. "Not that it matters." She rolled her hand in a "continue" gesture.

"Do you know Bogmall?" Keir asked suspiciously.

"I've met her once," Carver admitted. "She makes an impression."

"That she does." I winced. "It's hard to forget someone who keeps trying to kill you."

Carver's eyes widened, deepening the creases in his forehead. "And the last time was through possession?"

"If that was the last time." I didn't know if she was responsible for my magic going crazy today or not, but she was at the top of my suspect list. "But yes, she used anima-craft to inhabit the body of a fire witch, then tried to kill me. Again."

He pursed his lips for a moment, then said, "The last time we met, Bogmall was a druid chieftain. She was not a tru-craft witch. Did something change?"

"I'll say," Luanne snorted. "Bitch turned sorcerer."

Carver looked interested. "You mean she used ritual sacrifice to get her powers?"

"It's called murder these days," Lu interjected.

I nodded. "And she's not done yet."

Keir crossed his arms over his chest. "Bogmall is cunning and tenacious. From what we can tell, she killed a spirit witch in Nevada and used her new power to force a fire witch to relocate herself and her child to another state just to mess with Iris."

I felt sick thinking about the blonde bitch nearly forcing me to kill an innocent woman—another single mom like myself. On top of that, her daughter had been dating my son. Michael was handsome and charming like his father, so the cheerleader dating him could've been a coincidence. However, the chill that ran through my blood when I thought about how close my son had been to the horrible situation made me sick with worry.

"And you think she might be doing that again?" he asked. "If she has power already, it stands to reason she'd just move on. Why keep coming after Iris?"

"That's the million-dollar question," Lu said. "She's had a hard-on for Iris since day one."

I scrubbed my face to shake the trepidation. "She is like a volcanic pimple on picture day."

When Carver raised a quizzical brow, Marigold explained, "Guaranteed to show up and erupt at the most inconvenient time."

"Interesting." He tapped his chin, then held up a finger. "I might...yes." He nodded. "There just might be...."

"What are you thinking?" Thomas asked his younger friend.

"I don't know yet, but there's something...." His words trailed off as he lifted a hidden panel on the baggie side of his case and took out a piece of rough parchment and what looked like a drafting pencil. He sat at the breakfast bar and started to doodle and scribble.

I glanced at Thomas.

The man raised his bushy brows. "He was born with a gift for creative magic." He sounded oddly proud. "Give him a moment."

It dawned on me that there was something about Carver that had been troubling me since I'd first laid eyes on him, but until now, I hadn't been able to put my finger on it. I wasn't sure if the realization made me trust him more or less.

I pulled Keir aside and spoke quietly. "Bathroom," I told him.

"Now?" His eyes widened, and the creases at the corners went soft. "Why not?"

I elbowed him. "Not for that. I just want to talk to you out of ear shot of everyone."

"And if we have time, we could always...." He let the implication hang in the air.

I looped my arm in his and dragged him down the short hall and into the bathroom. There was a bottle of talcum powder on the back of the toilet. I twisted the top and squeezed a small amount in my palm. "Beyond these walls, no sound to hear. Within these walls, my words are clear." I clapped my hands together, scattering the dust around us. "There," I said. "We are soundproof now."

"Then I guess you can be as noisy as you want."

I chuckled. "This is serious."

Keir frowned, his gray eyes darkening. "What's wrong? I mean, other than the fact that someone is trying to get at you with magic."

I inhaled deeply and then let it out. "I'm not sure if this is something wrong or something right. It's more of an observation."

"What did you observe?"

"Unless I'm crazy, I think Carver is Thomas' son."

# CHAPTER 10

"No," Keir said. "Not Thomas." He shook his head and leaned against the counter. "The man is a confirmed bachelor. I've known him my whole life, and I can say with some certainty that I've never seen him involved romantically with anyone."

"Not every baby made is from a romantic encounter."

Keir tsked. "Nope. I would know if Thomas had a son. Especially if that son was close to my age. This is the first time I've ever met the man."

"Lu thinks Thomas and Freya are sleeping together."

"Lu is bitter and angry. Of course, she thinks they are lovers. While they do have a deep bond, their relationship isn't physical."

"You seem so sure of yourself," I said. I'll admit I was disappointed. I'd really thought I was on to something. Both Carver and Thomas were thin, had wild hair and bushy brows, and even their noses were similar. Coincidence? Maybe. But I swear I heard the pride in Thomas' voice. Like a father to a son or.... "Maybe I'm mistaking teacher-student pride for familial pride."

"Thomas wouldn't have been Carver's teacher. Their magic isn't the same. Thomas' craft is inherited. Carver is a practitioner, relying on the spell craft and rituals to create magic."

"Tru-craft witches use rituals and spell craft to do magic too."

"Yes, but you don't have to." Keir's fingers trailed down my arms. My skin tingled at his light touch. "That's the difference."

"But Thomas did say that his 'friend' had been born tru-craft but never sparked."

"True," Keir mused. "That doesn't mean he sired him."

"Considering Thomas is not a horse, I hope not." I sighed as I took a step forward, closing the distance between us, and sagged against Keir's body. "Maybe Carver is a nephew or something."

"Thomas doesn't have any siblings."

"A cousin then." There was an unpleasant whine in my tone. I didn't normally love gossip, especially considering I'd had a starring role in the gossip back home. I don't know why I wanted it to be true. Probably because I liked Thomas, and his potentially having a son made me feel like we were connected. Two tru-craft parents doing the best we could, or something to that effect. "It doesn't matter."

He brushed the hair back from my face with both of his hands. "I was scared earlier. I thought you were dying."

"Again?" I half-heartedly teased. "I don't die that easy."

"I know, but I can't see it anymore. Your futures are hidden from me, and now whenever anything happens, it feels like a movie I've watched but can't remember the ending."

I hated to admit it, but most of the time, I was glad he could no longer see all the possibilities all the time when it came to my life. He'd seen the hundreds of thousands of ways I lived, but he'd also seen all the ways that I could die. That wasn't a burden anyone should have to carry. The fact that he loved me made the visions all the more terrible. "Isn't that better? The not knowing or remembering."

I tilted my head back, my chin resting between Keir's collar bones. "Kiss me."

"The first sensible thing you've said since we got in here."

I lightly smacked his chest. "Make it quick before I change my mind."

He wrapped his arms around me and lifted me until my feet dangled and my lips were inches from his. "Challenge accepted."

Keir pressed his mouth to mine. At the swipe of his tongue, all thought left my brain and moved to other parts of my body as the kiss took on a frantic quality, lips pressed hard, splitting open and sending an electric pulse through me that I could feel down to my toes. He tasted chocolate and coffee. I mmmm'd my approval. My hands rubbed against the short shift of his hair, and he reciprocated, his fingers tangling in mine. I wrapped my legs around his waist as he carried me to the vanity and set me on the edge of the counter.

I slid my hand down between us, cupping his bulge and giving it a squeeze.

Keir growled against my lips. "Don't start something you're not ready to finish."

I popped the top button of his jeans open. "Oh, I'm ready."

"How long will your barrier last?"

I flexed my fingers toward the floor and twirled them in circles. "Stir and turn the air to churn." A light breeze stirred in the room, and I smiled. "We have time."

"His hands slid down my back until he cupped my ass, and his mouth slanted over mine as he teased me with licks and flicks of his tongue. I looped my fingers behind his neck, pulling him down into a crushing kiss that said, *I am yours. You are mine.*

Keir nudged my thighs wider, rubbing his groin against mine. He expertly angled his hips so that I felt every bit of length. Wet heat throbbed at my core, and I moaned against his mouth. I let out a noise of protest when he shifted away from me, then slid his hand over my stomach and slid his fingers down my pants.

I sucked in a breath and arched, and the back of my head bumped into the mirror when he deftly rubbed my swollen clit between two fingers. I rocked my hips forward, urging him to continue. A loud groan of pleasure escaped me, and I was thankful for the sound barrier.

"Ho, damn," I muttered as he slid my leggings and panties off. We were in a small bathroom with a crowd of people not more than twenty feet away. Making out was fun, but actually having sex gave me pause. "I'm not sure...."

Keir's mouth joined his fingers, and all doubt fled along with my good sense. I braced myself on the counter to keep from falling off the edge. Keir, without missing a lick, lifted my legs over his shoulders to keep me from sliding off the vanity.

He flicked his tongue in a way that made me gasp and grab for purchase, carelessly sending a tray of toiletries crashing to the floor. Keir was relentless in his pursuit of my ecstasy, and it didn't take much more than a few thrusts of his tongue inside me, as his teeth lightly grazed my sensitive nub, before I was drowning in burning pleasure.

I swung my hand out again to brace as the overwhelming orgasm shattered me from the inside with an achingly sweet release. Keir didn't stop until I stopped moving against his mouth, and he drank down the last of my climax.

He kissed his way up my stomach as he eased my legs off his shoulders. He wore the smug smile of a man who knew how to satisfy.

The corner of my mouth tugged up in a lazy smile. "Give me a second to recover, and I'll happily reciprocate."

Keir gave me a light kiss and whispered. "Save that thought for later."

"Why wait for later—"

A sharp clearing of a voice behind the door made me sit up straight. Shoot. For a hot second, I'd forgotten where we were and the audience nearby. On top of that, the breeze I'd stirred in the room had died down. Son of a gun.

"Hey, Carver has something," Luanne said from the other side of the door. "Finish up and get your asses out here."

I hopped to my feet and yanked on my pants. The room reeked of juniper and alcohol. Broken glass was on the tile. I'd broken a cologne bottle when I'd knocked crap off the counter. "Son of a biscuit," I hissed.

Keir chuckled as he picked up the shards.

I turned on the hot water tap and grabbed a wash-cloth from a small shelf against the wall. "It's not funny," I said.

Keir shrugged as he tossed the pieces into the trash. "It's a little funny."

I wiped down the counter as Keir picked up a shaving soap tin, a razor, and the bottle of talcum. Thankfully, I'd remembered to close the top before I'd set it down.

"We're going to need a broom and a mop for the floor." I washed my hands, lathering the soap before letting the water run over them. I tried to feel a connection to the clear liquid, the same as I had every day since the nero-craft symbol appeared on my grimoire, but there was nothing. The druids were going to test me on four elements. I was so screwed. I finished rinsing and then dried my hands on a nearby towel.

"I've made a real mess of things," I said.

Keir's eyes were hard with disbelief. "None of this is your fault." He took my hand and kissed my palm. "Your path was set for you long before you were born. It was handed down in your DNA, Iris. You are nothing short of remarkable."

"You have to say that because you love me," I said.

Keir washed his hands, dried them, then wrapped his arms around me. "I love you," he replied. "But that doesn't stop me from seeing the truth. In a short time, you have battled foes that would've crushed anyone else. Even witches who have trained their whole lives. You have faced every challenge with the courage of a warrior."

"I'm not sure I'd go that far. Not unless warriors are afraid all the time."

"We are," Luanne said through the door. "Now hurry up."

I let out a soft "oh," and then giggled.

Keir hugged me. "I know you're worried about water. We'll figure it out."

I hadn't been worried about sparking to nero-craft. I figured it would happen in its own good time, but time was no longer a luxury I had on my side. What kind of test would they give me? And what would happen if I couldn't pass? The not knowing gave me gas. "I hope so because the alternative is too awful to think about." I straightened my hair and smoothed my clothes. My cheeks were flushed, and I worried they screamed, this woman just had an orgasm. I turned to Keir. "Do I look okay?"

He smiled. "You're beautiful."

The compliment sent a zing through me. It was a heady feeling being loved and adored. "Not what I meant but thank you."

We left the bathroom and closed the door behind us. When I saw Thomas, I said, "You should probably call housekeeping."

"I'm housekeeping," he replied.

"Then you'll have to show me where you keep your mop."

He squinted at me. "Did you let loose a tornado in there?"

The heat of a blush rose in my cheeks. "Something like that."

Thomas gestured toward the breakfast bar where Luanne, Marigold, and Carver were standing. Fair Konig, his wings a blur, hovered over the top, and Linda stood on the counter.

"It is about time, *Kleinkind*," Linda chided. "I swear you'll be the death of me."

"Probably the death of all of us," Lu muttered.

"Hey," I protested.

Marigold smacked her for me. "Be nice."

I ignored the three of them. I walked over to Carver and looked down at his drawing. It was an elaborate mess of lines, circles, something that looked like handlebars, and a few squiggles. It was all Greek to me. "What did you figure out?"

"Ever heard of a PKE Meter?" Carver asked.

I smirked. "Ghostbusters?"

Carver grinned. "Nerd."

"Takes one to know one," I countered. In the movies, the PKE was a handheld device used to detect the presence of ghosts and spirits. I stared at Carver in awe. The man was a genius. "Are you going to build me a psychokinetic meter?" I was probably more excited than a forty-three-year-old woman should be about a fictional appliance. "Please tell me you are going to build me one."

He grinned. "I'm going to build you one."

# CHAPTER 11

IT TURNED OUT THE PKE METER WAS MORE OF A precious stone bracelet than a gadget. Luckily, Thomas had black tourmaline, obsidian, and jasper, three of the stone Carver said were "in tune with the spirit." He also needed peridot, a yellow-green semi-precious stone that Thomas didn't own, for balancing the energy.

"I have one," Marigold offered. She slid the peridot ring off her finger that our mother had given her for her eighteenth birthday.

"No," I told her. "I can't let you do this." Marigold was born in August, so the peridot was her birthstone. On top of that, the color complimented her light olive skin tone. After Mom's death, my sister never took off the ring. Its sentimental value far surpassed its cost. "That's asking too much."

With no hesitation, Marigold pressed the ring into my palm. "Losing you would be asking too much. This." She closed my fingers over the small piece of jewelry. "This I can lose."

If I hadn't known her so well, I wouldn't have glimpsed the pain she tried to hide. Giving up the ring wasn't as easy as she'd let on, but I wouldn't diminish her sacrifice by calling her out. "Thank you."

She let go of my hand and nodded. "You're welcome."

Carver curled his fingers in a "gimme" gesture. I handed him the ring. He held it up to the overhead light to examine the stone. "Perfect," he said. His gaze pivoted to Marigold. "And the good news is that I won't have to dismantle the ring to use it. I'll incorporate it like a charm. When Iris no longer needs it, you will have it back in one piece."

Marigold, who had been steeling her expression, let out a soft sigh of relief. Her eyes glistened with unshed tears. "That would be great."

"Now," Carver said as he pocketed the ring. "I just need an anchor stone."

"Like what?" Keir asked.

Linda snapped her fingers. "I have just zee thing." She hopped down from the counter and disappeared into the floor. Since we were on the second story, I wondered if she was surprising someone below by falling through.

I pushed the stones around on the counter. "To be clear, the bracelet won't actually protect me, right? How will I know if it's working?"

"The stones will grow uncomfortably warm, and they will vibrate," Carver answered.

Before I could ask more, Linda was back, holding a smooth, bleached rock with a hole in the center. My arms went up to block my face before I realized she wasn't going to throw it at me.

"Stupid, *Kleinkind*," she spat. "It is an anchor stone for the charm. I am not going to throw it at you."

"Can I help it if you've turned me into Pavlov's dog? I see a rock in your hand, and my first instinct is to block or duck."

She spun herself up onto the breakfast bar and set the stone down. "Give me fewer reasons to throw things at you, and you will stop anticipating the blows."

"I have a feeling you'd find a reason to pelt me no matter how good I was."

Carver stuck the tip of his pinky into the hole in the rock. "A hag stone." He admired the shape. "It's perfect."

Linda happily tugged her beard. "I saw it earlier by a stream that runs through the woods."

I gave her a sharp look. "The warrior told me about your vision from last night. I wanted to check out the property to see if there was any evidence left behind."

"And was there?"

"Not that I could find," she said. "Fair Konig's search was as fruitless as well."

Fair Konig's wings made a buzzing sound as he darted back and forth like a hummingbird on sugar water. "I'm sorry, Iris Everlee. I have failed you."

"You haven't," I told him. "Whatever I saw was shown to me from a past event. Something that took place a long time ago. For what reason? That remains to be seen, but I would've been more surprised if you or Linda had found something tangible."

Carver closed his case. "It'll take me a few hours to etch the stones and bind them into a protection wrap. I need a neutral room to craft in. Something that holds neither negative nor positive energy."

"That excludes the bathroom," Lu snarked.

I gave her a slight shove. She was ready for it and didn't budge.

Thomas shook his head, but his eyes were lit with mirth. "I have a spelling chamber in my bedroom."

"You're bedroom, huh?" I asked with sudden interest.

"I don't need a walk-in closet," Thomas said in his defense. "So, I turned it into a workspace." He turned to Carver. "It's carbon-lined, and I had it smudged a week ago. I haven't used it since."

"That'll work." The eclectic witch gathered his gear into his arms. "Show me the way."

Interesting. I still thought the connection between them was more than friends, but Keir seemed pretty sure about Thomas' personal life or lack thereof.

When the two men left the room, Marigold broke the silence. "I'm starving. Who do I have to bribe to get some snacks around here?"

"I know who," Lu said.

"If she takes you out into the middle of a maze, don't drink the wine."

The warrior druid pressed her fingertips against her chest. "Ouch. That hurts."

"The truth often does." I chuckled. "Go. Feed my sister. Bring her back unscathed."

"What if I want to get a little scathed?" Marigold asked.

"Tough. No scathing allowed."

Luanne laughed. "You're such a party pooper, Iris."

"Every party needs one." I waved as Lu led my sister out of the apartment. I had a feeling Luanne had been itching to get out since before she'd arrived. Although, I thought she'd been on her best behavior. For my sake? Maybe. For Carver's sake... He didn't seem like her type, but honestly, I had no idea what Luanne's type was, unlike my sister, who liked them scorching hot. Literally.

Speaking of hot. "Have you heard from Zev?" I asked Keir.

"I haven't spoken to him since the pixie mating frenzy weekend," he answered. "Why?"

"I'm being tested on my magic. Linda is my earth guardian, Fair Konig is my air guardian, and Zev is my fire guardian. I have two of the three here. I'm reluctant to ask, but should he be here too?"

"It's not a bad idea to have him around. He's connected to you in a way that doesn't require the usual quid pro quo. Why are you reluctant to ask?"

"Marigold, duh." I scrubbed my cheeks. "She's really into the fiery ifrit, and I'm afraid she's going to get burned. Not a metaphor."

"I get it, but Zev won't let it get that far."

"I like the guy, but I don't trust him with my sister's heart. He plays it hot and cold when he's around her, no pun intended. She acts like she's tough, but Marigold goes all in when she catches feelings for someone." I only wished she had better taste in men. She was educated, beautiful, and a total boss. Unfortunately, she liked her men hot, unpredictable, and dangerous. Zev was all three of those things. Luckily, she usually knew when to get out while the getting was good.

"I still think it's a good idea to call him. Your magic is more stable when your guardians are close at hand."

I laughed at that notion. "Oh, how I wish that were true."

"I've been thinking on it," Keir said. "I wonder if the way each element has sparked is its way of finding your guardian. Maybe that's why your nero-craft hasn't manifested yet. You need a water guardian."

"Didn't you mention a sea hag you knew from up north?"

"Sea witch," Keir corrected, then quickly added, "Not her."

I gave him a wary glance. "Is there some history I should know about?"

He shrugged. "Only if you really want to know."

That wasn't the response I'd expected. I tried to recall the conversation surrounding the sea witch. Luanne had been the one who had called her a sea hag. Her name was Malphista, and Lu had called her Malfeasant. She hated the witch. I wasn't sure if it was because of something the sea hag had done to Keir or to herself. Even so, I had to ask myself, did I really want to know about his past with other women? And on the same note, did I want him to know everything about my past with other men?

The response to both those questions was, "Nope. I'm good. Sea hag is a no-go."

"Good answer," Keir said.

"Still, I really need to find a water guardian to get my mojo rising, so to speak."

"Your mojo is fine for now."

"Yeah, but what happens when the high-druid mucky-mucks start testing me on it? I wasn't worried or in a hurry to spark, but it feels urgent now."

"True." Keir narrowed his gaze and stared toward the French doors to the balcony.

"Your wheels are spinning."

"Huh?" He blinked at me. "What?"

"Your wheels," I reiterated. "They are a spinnin'. What are you thinking?"

"I'm thinking there has to be a way to find out what tests they plan to employ."

"Is that considered cheating?"

"Only if you get caught."

"You strike me as a rule follower," I told him.

He smirked, his gray eyes alight with mischief. "Then you have not been paying attention."

I snorted a laugh. "I pay attention." But he wasn't wrong. I knew in my heart Keir would break every rule necessary to keep me safe, and I wanted nothing more than to let him. Still, I worried about the trouble he'd get into with his people on my behalf. "I don't want you risking your life in the Iron Grove because of me."

"Oh, Iris." He wrapped me in his arms and held me close. "How many times do I have to tell you before you believe me? I don't care about having a life that doesn't include you. I'd give up the Iron Grove and all its inhabitants, and I mean all of them if it meant you'd never have to suffer again. The offer to run away is still on the table if you're game. We could leave right now and never look back."

"Only if you've figured out how we're going to disappear with my entire family in tow...."

Keir kissed the top of my head. "Then it's plan B."

"Plan B?"

"Operation Sneak Peek."

I grinned and tilted my head back to kiss his jaw. "Clever."

"I thought so." He gave my ass a sharp slap that I honestly didn't mind and said, "Ready for some spy games?"

"This seems more like a Lu special."

"I'm more than capable of stealth," he replied. "Quit stalling, and let's go."

I gave his butt a reciprocal slap when he let me go and turned toward the front door. "Okay, Double-O-SexyAss." As he sauntered to the exit, I added, "Shake it, don't stir it."

I blushed hotly as he looked back over his shoulder with a heated gaze that promised all kinds of pleasure. "You coming?"

"Not yet, but the night looks promising."

He shook his head. "Incorrigible. I love that about you."

I let out a low whistle as I pulled my libido up from the floor and followed him out of the apartment.

# CHAPTER 12

WE USED THE BACK SERVANTS' HALLWAYS AND staircases, and I recognized the paths from the night before when Luanne had led me down to the hedge maze.

The Iron Grove was druid ran, and druid maintained, so there weren't any actual servants on the compound, but I can see why the person who designed and built the place thought the private entrances and exits might be needed.

"This must've been a lot of fun when you were kids," I said.

Keir nodded. "Lu and I didn't spend a lot of time here. We were mostly on the road with Dad. His work took us all over the world. But the few times we visited Freya, we made these back hallways our playground." He stopped and gestured to a chipped-out line of millwork, thigh height on the wall. "That's where Lu tackled me into the wall and broke my front tooth."

"Ouch."

He touched his tooth. "Thomas called in a terra-craft practitioner to regrow it. Even so, it always felt loose in the socket...until I became a puca. The first time I transformed, when I became human again, the tooth was like brand new."

He'd told me that he'd gone on a quest to become a supernatural beast, to become someone who could protect me. I had so many questions about the how and why of it all, but Keir had seemed ashamed, for lack of a better word, or even a little horrified that I'd seen him in his big scary bunny form, so I never pressed him. But since he'd brought it up....

"You never told me what you had to do to become the puca."

"Nope," he agreed. "I haven't."

"If you don't want to talk about it, that's fine. I get it. There are things I'd soon forget too."

He put his arm around my shoulder as we continued down the hall. "I don't know how you can so easily accept the monster I have become."

"You can't be serious." I scoffed. "Other than the gnarly teeth, the black diamond claws, and the glossy black eyes, you're kind of cute when you go all," I made my hands into claws, "*grrrrrr*."

Keir chuckled. "You're too much."

"That's not the first time I've heard that."

He squeezed me sideways, and I almost tripped over my own feet.

"Do you know puca lore?"

"Some," I admitted. "I did my fair share of internet searching after you took down the gargoyle."

He snickered. "I'm not surprised."

"I like to learn things," I told him. "I've always been

that way. If it's any consolation, there wasn't a whole lot of information out there on the inter-web."

He let go of me and stopped in front of one of the many doors we'd passed that led to various rooms in the house. "This goes to the kitchen," he said. "It's after seven, so it should be empty."

I think he forgot that Luanne and Marigold had gone on a quest for snacks. "I bet we'll find a couple of sisters lurking about."

"Luckily, they aren't the ones we're hiding from."

"Damn." I gaped at the ginormous kitchen as we exited the hall. I didn't know much about high-end appliances, but a dual oven with dual gas ranges looked pricey. There was a refrigerator that looked bigger than my ensuite and four cabinet-mounted microwaves that were bigger than my oven. Even with all the fancy equipment, there was still warmth to the kitchen. The cabinets were cream-colored with pops of sage green. The marble counters were the same cream with veins of gray and green. And taking up space was a center island that could easily seat twelve people. Right now, it seated five.

Marigold, Luanne, Simon, Harry, and Hellie were talking and laughing as they built sandwiches Dagwood would've been jealous of. Dagwood Bumstead had been a character in a comic strip series. Dad would always give my siblings and me the comic section of the Sunday paper. We'd lay it out on the ground, and we'd all read it together. The character was always making stacked sandwiches that were too big for a human to consume, but it hadn't stopped us from trying.

I smiled at the memory.

Luanne noticed us first. "Hey! You all made it down." She waved us over. "You're just in time to see Harry attempt to take a bite of this monster sandwich Marigold has built. If any of the inside drops to the counter, he loses."

"What's the bet?" I asked.

"If he loses, he pays for dinner at a nice restaurant of my choosing, and if he wins, then I pay," Marigold said.

I quirked a brow at Harry. "It sounds like Harry wins no matter the outcome."

He grinned at me. "You got me there." He took a bite of the sandwich, and a piece of bacon dropped to the counter. The other druids vocalized their disappointment with a collective "aww." But Harry looked like the cat who ate the canary as he finished chewing. He gave my sister a wink. "I guess I'm buying dinner." The rascal. He'd made sure he lost. I liked Harry. He seemed like a really nice guy. Which meant he didn't stand a chance with Marigold. Still, I applauded his efforts.

Simon, his blond hair pulled back in a ponytail, cut a hunk off the end of the stacked sub. He gestured with it toward Keir and me. "You guys want in on this?"

It looked good, but I was still feeling nauseated from my earlier run-in with spirit magic. "Thanks, but I'll pass. You guys enjoy."

Hellie waved a bottle of wine at me. "You need a little hair of the dog that bit you."

I shook my head. "That dog needs to be put down," I told her. "It has rabies."

"Iris!" Marigold gasped. "Not the dog. Never the dog."

"Fine." I harrumphed. "That dog needs some serious obedience training, and it isn't going to get it from me."

"Spoilsport," Hellie said.

"I get that a lot."

"Hey," Harry quipped. "Did you know that Marigold took out a satyr?"

I gave my sister a WTF look and told him, "I was there when it happened."

"So, it's true?" Simon's eyes widened with mild shock.

Marigold threw a tomato slice at him. "Did you think I was lying?"

He shrugged, then all the druids, except Keir, laughed. My sister kept her gaze averted from mine. She was telling tales, and I wasn't sure I wanted these near strangers knowing all our business, but the satyr story had been hers to tell. It was probably nice for her to have people she could talk to openly about real magic and monsters.

"Just make sure the stories are yours to tell." The embarrassed flush in her cheeks made me sorry I said it. "I'm sorry. You know what I mean."

"I do." She stuck her tongue out at me and crossed her eyes. It was as close as I was going to get to her letting me off the hook for being rude.

Keir took that as our cue to leave. "You guys have fun," he said. "Don't get into too much trouble."

Luanne gave her brother a thumbs up. "Back at ya."

Keir grabbed my hand and guided me through the kitchen and into the formal dining room. It was pristinely clean. There wasn't a crumb or a hair on the table. There was a fireplace and mantle that was dusted within an inch of its life, and there was zero evidence that there had ever been a fire in the insert. Even the giant crystal chandelier was sparkly and dust free.

"This room never gets used," Keir said.

"I can tell."

I thought about Marigold, a human, hanging out with druids. Was that okay? Was it safe to leave her alone with people used to fighting the supernatural? Marigold, as she'd told her new friends, had managed to take down a satyr. She chopped his head off with a shovel to stop it from killing me. Hell, the first time she'd met Zev, she'd launched herself at him on my front porch and tried to attack him because she thought he was there to hurt me. My sister was foolishly brave when it came to my well-being. Her willingness to run headfirst into danger was part of my worry.

As if reading my mind, Keir said, "Marigold will be fine. Luanne will take care of her."

"The way she took care of me last night?"

He sighed. "She'll be extra careful because of last night."

"I know." The knowledge didn't erase my unease. I'd been so glad that Keir had invited her to come, but that was before I knew somebody was actively trying to mess with me. If it had been simply a matter of the archdruids testing me, Marigold would be in no danger. However, if Bogmall had a hand in the spirit spell cast on me last night, I knew she would use every weakness against me, including my love for my sister. Even if the blonde sorcerer wasn't involved, someone had tried to make my magic turn against me. I couldn't protect Marigold. I could barely protect myself.

Simon caught up to us at a jog. "A little bird told me to let you know that the covens are building Iris's tests around the henge inside the maze." He tapped his nose. "You didn't hear it from me. I'm late for rounds. Talk later."

He left us at a jog and disappeared around a corner.

"Who do you think the little bird is?" I asked.

"If I had to guess, I'd say it was my grandmother. Simon is the head of her security, and he's been with her for over twenty years."

Basically, his whole entire adult life. "Wow. So, you think we can trust the information?"

Simon had been the one to give me the wine goblet the night before, after all. He could be possessed by Bogmall, and we'd never know until she showed her cards. I rubbed my wrist. I'd feel a lot better about all of this once Carver finished my bracelet.

"I don't trust anyone but you right now."

I squeezed his hand. "Same. Well, Bob. I trust Bob, too."

Keir smiled. "Of course." He gave me a steady look. "Do you want to risk checking out the maze? Or we can go back to the room and wait for Carver to finish his work."

"I want to know," I told him. "Besides, the only reason she got to me last night was that I hadn't expected to be attacked here at the Iron Grove. I won't make that mistake again. On top of that, I have a giant, scary wabbit to protect me."

Keir shook his head. "We'll stay out of sight. No one will even know we're there."

Famous last words.

After we stealthily made our way through the maze, I was aghast at the work the coven of tru-craft witches were doing. There was a monolith boulder ten feet high and at least four feet in diameter on the east side of the henge. To the north was a wind funnel, carrying debris into its grasp. Two witches held it in place with a murmured chant. To the south was a pile of logs stacked against a standing pole. Egads, were they planning on burning me at the stake? And to the west....

"What the hell is that contraption?"

"It's a water vault," a man said from behind us.

I jumped and gave a sharp yip as we both pivoted to face the Green Grove leader Derrick Asher.

He smiled genially. "I'm glad my message was passed along."

"You're the one who told Simon about where to find the tests?" Keir asked.

Derrick Asher had jumped to the top of my suspect list for Bogmall's possession. Oh, how I wished I had the bracelet already. The bitch was not going to play her hand in front of Keir, but I would make sure Derrick was the first person who got a handshake from me as soon as Carver finished the charm.

However, I didn't want him to know that I suspected him of being a murderous, power-hungry *Hexenmeister*. "What is a water vault?" I asked, changing the subject.

"What it sounds like." Derrick's expression was forlorn. "They will put you in there and lock the top. The water will fill up until there is no room for air, and you will have to find a way to escape using your nero-craft."

Well, I was fucked.

"And how am I supposed to do that? I'm not freaking Houdini."

"Houdini died doing the water vault escape," Derrick said.

I glared at him. "Well, that's terrible."

"He didn't actually die from the water torture trick. He had sepsis from peritonitis or a burst appendix. There is some disagreement among scholars," Keir acknowledged.

My guy taught a class on the supernatural and the occult at Darling University. Houdini had been a big believer in the occult and had spent a lot of money on mediums trying to prove the afterlife existed. Which meant he was probably part of Keir's curriculum.

However, I wasn't sure knowing his true means of death made me feel any better.

I pressed my hands against my stomach. "I'm going to throw up." Forget Bogmall. The witch test was going to accomplish what she couldn't. It was going to kill me.

"I'm sorry," Derrick said with so much sincerity it made me want to punch him. "I thought knowing what you were up against would make the fight less terrifying."

Yeah, sure, he did. "Mission failed," I muttered, then I vomited at the base of the nearest hedge.

# CHAPTER 13

I WRAPPED MY HAIR IN A TOWEL AFTER MY SHOWER AND then immediately flopped on the bed in our room.

Marigold sat in a lemon-yellow puffy chair near the window, her bare feet propped up on a matching pouf as she played on her phone. "Do you need help?"

"No. I feel better now." My nausea had passed as quickly as it had come. I'd had to reassure Keir all the way back to our room to keep him from sweeping me off my feet and carrying me to bed. In a romance novel, that was the stuff of fantasies. In real life, it felt more like damsel-in-distress syndrome.

"Maybe we should call a doctor," Marigold said. "You sound like you have a concussion."

"That would require getting hit in the head," I told her. "But I don't have any head trauma."

"That you know of." She snapped. "You need to stop taking chances with your life. You're not a cat. You don't get nine of them."

Bob jumped up on the bed and curled into my arms.

"She wasn't talking about you, chonky-chonk." I gave him a hug and rubbed my face against his fur. His purring instantly relaxed me. "Such a sweet, good boy," I told him. "The goodest."

Marigold went back to her phone. "Did you know that Houdini's water torture chamber weighed 7000 pounds and could hold up to 250 gallons of water?"

"Why are you looking that up? Are you trying to torture me?"

My sister set her phone down. "I thought it was interesting."

"Here's something interesting for you. In the next couple of days, I'm going to be placed in a real-life water torture chamber."

She pulled her legs up onto the seat and tucked her feet under her thighs. "I think you should opt-out."

"Hah." As if that were a choice. "I'm afraid opting out isn't on the board."

"Luanne told me that if you chose to forego the testing, the covens would bind your powers." She met my gaze, her dark brown eyes serious with her conviction. "Let them bind your powers."

"No." I shook my head. "I won't let them. Not without a fight."

"Isn't being like the rest of us mere mortals better than dying?"

My powers had become such an integral part of my identity of late I wasn't sure if it was better. I mean, obviously, dying was super bad and to be avoided at all costs. But I wasn't ready to concede my magic yet.

Marigold hit me where it hurt. "What about Michael?

Are you ready to leave him in a world without his mom? You and I both know what that's like. Are you ready for your son to experience pain so deep it never completely goes away?"

I sighed as I stroked Bob's thick fur. My sister was right. I had to think about more than my own feelings. I would hate it, but I could live without magic if I had to— the operative word being *live*. "If I don't think I can survive one of the tests, I will quit the trials."

"Promise?" Marigold asked.

I let go of my imp-cat and sat up on the bed. "I promise."

Those two words seemed to appease my sister for the moment as she reclined back and picked up her phone again. "Oh my gosh. They would lower him into the chamber headfirst. Can you imagine?"

I could imagine all too well, and the thought of it made my stomach roil again. "Please stop reading about Houdini."

Marigold set her phone down again. "I'm just trying to help."

It suddenly dawned on me that Keir hadn't called my sister for her company alone. In all the chaos over being spelled, I'd forgotten about the one thing he asked her to bring that might give me a clue as to how to pull my butt out of this disaster.

"Do you have my grimoire?"

"Oh, yeah," she said. "It's out in the car."

A myriad of emotions ran through me, with the prevailing one being alarm. "You left it in the car? What if someone breaks in and steals it?"

"No one's going to steal it," she protested.

I grimaced. "You do know that the grimoire is sentient, right?" I'd hidden and locked it away in my crawlspace attic once, and I don't think it had forgiven me yet. "It is not going to like being forgotten like old fast-food wrappers in the back of your car."

"I'll have you know that I treated it like anything important I want to leave in the car. I stuck it under some towels in the backseat like I would my purse or my laptop. No one will even know it's there."

"Please don't tell me you leave your purse in the car unattended."

"Okay." She shrugged. "I won't tell you that I leave my purse in the car, under a towel, unattended."

"But you do."

"Damn, right, I do. That thing gets heavy if I have to lug it around all day."

"Try putting fewer things in it."

Her mouth dropped open, and her eyes widened. "How dare you?"

I chuckled. "You always know how to make me feel better."

She smiled and tucked back in the chair again. "It's a gift. Should I go get your book?"

"That would be awesome. But you probably shouldn't go out in the dark by yourself."

"Keir left strict orders that you were to stay in the room until he got back."

"Since when do you let a guy dictate what you do?"

"Since I agree with him. Until Carver finishes that charm bracelet, you need to keep yourself safe." She wiggled her way to the edge of the seat and got up. "And don't worry. I didn't say a word about Bog-bitch, spirit magic, and possessions earlier to the druids. I know how to keep my mouth shut."

"I'm glad you had a chance to talk about stuff with people in the know. I'm sorry if I sounded like I was calling you out. I'm scared, and it manifests as bitchiness. I shouldn't take it out on you."

"When monsters, people, and magic stop trying to harm you, you can write me a long apology letter. Until then, we're cool. Maybe I can get Linda to go out to the car with me."

"If you can find her." I hadn't seen neither hide nor stone of the gnome since we'd left Thomas' apartment. Fair Konig, either. "I'm sure that she and the pixie king are up to no good somewhere."

"You know Linda worships the ground you walk on, right?"

I blew a raspberry. "Only if stoning is a form of prayer."

"For Linda, it's her love language."

I rubbed my forehead, completely healed now, out of habit. "She could stand to love me a little less."

"You don't mean it."

I shook my head. "No, I don't mean it. I do want my grim, though. I'm sure it will give me a cryptic poem that I won't be able to decipher and will only make sense once I save myself."

Marigold snorted a laugh. "It sounds frustrating. Why bother?"

"Because the undecipherable message means that all

hope isn't lost. There's still a way forward, even when I can't see it." I got up and took the towel off my head. My hair was damp but not drenched. It was fine enough that it wouldn't take long to dry.

"That actually makes a lot of sense." She stood up and brushed her cream-colored flowy pants down, and straightened her purple floral tunic top. "Do you want me to go get it or not?"

"Not without a buddy," I told her.

"Who would you suggest? It's not like I can phone a friend."

"Text Luanne."

Marigold took up her phone again. "This seems really silly. My car is parked in the attached garage. I wouldn't even have to leave the house to go get the silly thing."

"Humor me," I said. "It will make me feel better knowing you have someone with you who has your back." I got up and went to the dresser. "You know, the way you always have mine."

"I'll escort Marigold to her vehicle."

Marigold yelped as we both shot a look at the ifrit who had just materialized in the middle of the room. I tripped over the hem of my robe, smacked the corner of my forehead against the dresser, and let out a string of colorful expletives.

"Damn it, Zev!"

"My apologies, *sahira*." He wore dark blue denim jeans, motorcycle boots, and a black leather jacket. He bent at the waist in a low bow and moved his arm with a flourish. "Your man summoned me, so I made the assumption that you knew I would be arriving."

"Not in the middle of my room." I rubbed the knot on my head. "And not without any warning."

The dark-haired man crossed his arms over his chest and lowered his gaze to mine. "I was given no warning when I was commanded to appear."

Whoa. The ifrit was pissed. I'd never seen him angry before. At least not at me. "I'm sorry, Zev. You don't have to stay. You're not mine or Keir's to command."

"That's not exactly true. I'm your fire guardian. When you need me, I cannot ignore the call." He looked sullen and grumpy, which in turn made Marigold look lusty and horny.

Oh, for heaven's sake. "I didn't know that," I admitted. "I've only been at this tru-craft business for a few months, and no one has bothered to give me a rule book." Now, I sounded surly. I waved a hand at him. "Sorry."

Maybe Marigold was right. If I let the covens bind my magic, then Zev would no longer be tied to me. He'd told me once that a djinn's worst nightmare is enslavement. Had my powers tied him to me in a way that left him with no choice? Without my tru-craft, Linda and Fair Konig would be free of me as well. Would it break the bond between Keir and me? I always worried that I had an unfair advantage in our relationship. Would binding my magic put us on a level playing field?

"You got smoke coming out your ears," Marigold pointed out.

I automatically reached up and touched my ears.

"Not literally," she elaborated with a roll of her eyes. She turned to our swarthy guest. "Hello, Zev."

"Hello, Marigold," he replied. Unsurprisingly, he

sounded less angry talking to my sister. "I'm delighted to see you again."

I let out a noisy breath of protest. Sure, with Marigold, he was delighted.

Zev's dark eyes swirled with amber flames as he turned his attention back to me. "What will you have of me, *sahira*?"

My instinct was to go full-on pissy. I mean, my life was in major flux right now, and I didn't want to have to deal with Zev's feelings on top of my own. However, I realized it was a little bit like a boss asking an employee to work overtime for free, then expecting the employee to love all the extra work. In other words, this whole situation was unfair to Zev.

"I need you," I told him, trying to be as honest as possible without trying to guilt him or get angry. "The Iron Grove and North American druid council are going to bind my powers if I can't pass the *malificionito*. If I can't pass the trials for each element, the tests can turn me into *aether* dust, and if I refuse to take part in their little shit-show, then they are going to bind my magic, basically stripping me of tru-craft. My birthright."

The last word struck me as powerful. I had been born a witch but had been raised without any knowledge of my past. My craft tied me to an ancestry that I never imagined existed, filled with tru-craft witches who had survived persecution and witch hunts. I didn't want to lose that connection.

"I won't ask you to stay if you don't want to," I told the ifrit. "I'm not your master." I met his fiery gaze. "Though I had hoped I was your friend."

His angry stare softened to something less harsh. "I will escort your sister to her vehicle, and we will discuss strategy when I return."

I let go of the breath I hadn't realized I was holding. "Thank you, Zev."

He touched his forehead and gave a slight bow before pivoting to Marigold. "Shall we?"

She gave him a dazzling smile. "We shall." She looped her arm in his, and the two of them left.

After the door closed, I blew out a slow, noisy breath, then grabbed a pillow and screamed into it. Bob's purring ramped up to a ten as he crisscrossed between and around my legs, rubbing his fur against my skin.

"I'm fine," I told him. "I'm okay." But if that was true, then why was I crying? I swiped at my tears as they trailed down my cheeks. I felt like the most selfish person in the room, always making everything about me. But in this case, it was about me. Whatever happened over the next two days, the odds weren't in my favor.

I sat on the edge of the bed, wallowing in my pity-party for one. I dabbed tears from my eyes, then rubbed my wet fingertips together and sniffed. "Pull yourself together, Iris." Falling apart, for me, was a solo sport. It was a side of myself that I didn't show to anyone, not if I could help it. I didn't want Keir or Marigold to see me so distraught. They were both worried enough already. I didn't want them to know how truly afraid I felt.

"Stupid tears." They were slick and thick, like the artificial ones that come from the store. Which meant I was dehydrated. "I really need to drink more water," I muttered.

I lifted my hand, suddenly fascinated by the glistening of tears on my skin. The way the liquid sunk into every swirl and whorl on my fingers. "What the..." I jerked my chin toward my chest when I noticed the tears that I'd wiped from my face seemed to be traveling toward my fingertips. Was I imagining this? Had I hit my head harder than I'd thought? Or was it real?

I concentrated on the fluid and tried to move it with my mind in a different direction. My energy was wasted. The tears kept going until they gathered in points on my fingertips. I held my hand out. Crap. If this was my magic, it was definitely wild. Was I going to turn into a puddle of water? After all, I'd turned crusty with earth magic, turned to lava with fire, and air magic had disappeared half my body. Crap. Crap. Knowing my luck, I'd get wiped up with a towel and thrown into the laundry. And then what? Washed out to some gray water tank. It was too horrible to think about.

Or was this someone else's magic? My eyes widened as the points of water began to sway and dance. Had Bogmall claimed another tru-craft witch's powers? This time a water witch? I got up, cinched my robe, and slipped on some flip-flops. I had to find Keir. Or better yet, Thomas. Something freaky was happening to me, and I didn't want to be alone in case it took me over.

I hustled to the door, opened it and staggered back as I faced Thomas on the other side.

"You about gave me a heart attack," I said. "But I'm so glad you're here." I held up my water-spiked fingers. "I think my nero-craft has sparked."

Thomas looked upset but not surprised as he stepped

aside to reveal Carver standing behind him. His hazel blue eyes had turned to orbs of clear blue water. "What's wrong with him?"

"You," Thomas said without accusation. "This is your doing."

# CHAPTER 14

"I don't understand," I said. "How is this my doing?" One of these days, I was going to stop asking that question. Every element of my magic had brought about major consequences to someone or something other than myself. With tera-craft, I'd cracked a community swimming pool while it was filled with children, including my nephews. With ignis-craft, I had awakened a self-proclaimed fire god from the magma layer of the Earth's core, and he'd threatened to level a mountain. And with aero-craft, I'd triggered a pixie mating ritual eight hundred years before it was scheduled to take place. So, the logical question, as I stared in horror at Carver's unseeing eyes, was, how wasn't this my fault?

Thomas ushered Carver, who seemed to be in a catatonic state, inside the room. I quickly closed the door behind them.

"Is he okay?" This should've been my first question, but I had been having my own freakout prior to their arrival. I held up my hands. "Are his eyes balls of water because of this?" The tears on my fingertips swirled like mini-cyclones. "I don't know why this is happening."

"When did that start?" Thomas asked.

"A minute or less before you showed up. How long ago did Carver's eyes turn?"

Thomas nodded as if that confirmed his hunch. "We were on the way to your room with the charm he made you. It happened as we were about twenty feet down the hall from your door."

"So, both events happened at the same time."

He scratched his head. "It would appear so." The wrinkles around his mouth turned into grooves as he frowned. "Can you think of any catalyst that might have precipitated the event?"

His clinical question about this metaphysical crapfest helped to calm the rising panic that welled inside me. "Not that I can think of.... Well, I was crying a little bit." I winged. "Okay. I was crying a lot. But in my defense, it's been a long day, and I was finally alone long enough to let it hit me."

"Did something else happen?"

"You mean other than spirit magic bursting from my forehead like a unicorn horn?"

"Yes, other than that."

"Well, let's see. I'd snuck down to see what kind of trials they had planned for me and found out they are going to try and burn me at the stake, and if that doesn't kill me, they are going to drown me in a water torture chamber." I pressed my hand against my stomach. "Then I puked a whole bunch." I snapped my fingers, and the tear-tornados danced away from getting squished. "Oh, yeah. Then I cried like a baby. But other than that...." I spread my hands before me, then closed my hands as the liquid spikes waggled.

I didn't even bother to mention that I might have been the reason for the servitude of a djinn who'd worked really hard to never be anyone's prisoner.

"The intense emotions must have sparked your nero-craft," Thomas said, his voice suddenly shaky. "It must have triggered Carver as well. We could ask Corina, a nero-craft witch from the Luna Grove coven. She might know how to help Carver through this transition."

He looked doubtful enough that I shook my head. "We can't trust any of the other groves or covens at this point. The ifrit Zev should be here in a few minutes. He's been around for a seriously long time, and he is an elemental through and through. He'll know what's happening to Carver."

Thomas took a relieved breath. "I hope you're right."

"Why is this happening to Carver? He's human, right? How is my magic turning a human into an elemental?"

"It couldn't," Thomas said. "If Carver was completely human, but he's not."

"That's right. You said he was born tru-craft but never sparked." However, Linda, Zev, and Fair Konig were all supernatural creatures born in symbiosis with the elements they embodied. Linda stone, Zev fire, and Fair Konig air. "I know I'm new to tru-craft, and I don't know all the rules, but how does a human become a water guardian? It doesn't make any sense."

The old witch's expression waffled between worry and grief. "His mother was a half-naiad, half sylph," Thomas said. "Lanastacia was the elemental who guided me when I first sparked to aero-craft."

"But if Carver's mother was a water elemental, how did she act as your guardian for air?"

"That was her sylph half. Sylphs are wind-born, but naiads are creatures of the water. Lanastacia carried both. She was a talented force of nature who saved my life more times than I can count."

"You loved her."

"I cared for her deeply, yes. Did I love her? In my own way, I suppose I did."

"But Carver is your son," I blurted out in a more "gotcha" tone than I'd intended. Oops. "I mean, he is, right?"

Thomas looked surprised then he shook his head before nodding once. "Yes, he is. How did you know?"

"You both look remarkably similar. The hair, the bone structure, the bushy brows."

"Lanastacia and I were only together once, and he was the product of our union." He peeped a sad smile. "He doesn't know about me."

If Carver had any awareness beneath his catatonia, he knew now. "Does he know about his mother?"

"No," Thomas said. "When he was born human, her people forced her to give him up. A nice family adopted him when he was barely a few days old."

The story had an itch of familiarity. My birth mother had abandoned me at the Briarberry Hospital when I was six months old. When Grace Everlee, my adopted mom, got the call about an abandoned baby girl who needed her, she and my dad drove all day to the other side of the mountain to pick me up. Fourteen months later, I officially became an Everlee. I didn't regret one minute of being my mom and dad's kid, but sometimes I wondered why my birth mother kept me for so long only to give me up. There had to have been a part of her that thought she could raise me.

"Why didn't you take him?" I instantly regretted asking, but it was a question I'd pondered off and on since I'd found out about tru-craft. "You don't have to answer. I'm sure you both did what you thought was best for him."

"I was unaware of his existence," Thomas said. Pain laced his words. "I would've found a way to make him a home if I'd been given a choice." His expression grew wistful. "I don't blame Lanastacia. She was doing her best to protect him and give him a normal life."

"How did you find out about him?"

"When the war came, she fought with the druids and my coven. With me and for me. An ignis-craft witch from the other side had a dragon for his guardian. He used the beast to mortally wound Lanastacia. She only told me about Carver when she was dying. She'd been checking on the boy for years, and she begged me to watch over him. I promised her I would." The old man's voice choked as he stared at his son. "I have failed."

Oh, man. I really was a monster. "This isn't your fault, Thomas." I walked over to Carver and examined him more closely. The tears that refused to dry swirled harder, tickling my fingertips. I shook my hands, but the tiny twists of liquid hung tight.

I strained against the pull as my hands were lifted by

the free-floating rivulets that treated me like a puppet on strings.

"Thomas?" I goggled at him. "Help."

Before he could react, my hands were on Carver's face, and the tears were seeping into his skin. The water drained from the eclectic witch's eyes as the white returned to his sclera and the color to his irises. His black pupils flexed and contracted as his sight readjusted.

He stared down at me. His expression was curious but relaxed. "That was really weird."

I smirked. "Tell me about it."

A throaty sob choked from Thomas.

"Oh." I went to the man, who, for the first time, appeared his age. Fear for his son had made him look old and frail. It made me think of my father back home, losing his sense of time and his memory, and I knew one day, in the near-ish future, I would lose him. Thomas was older than my dad.

I wanted to hug him, but he might not welcome the comfort.

Carver, surprising both of us, hugged the old witch instead. "It's okay, Thomas. I'm going to be just fine."

"I'm sorry, boy," Thomas said. "I never meant for you—"

"I've known for a long, long time." Carver leaned back and wiped Thomas' tears. I watched wide-eyed as those were also absorbed into his skin. "I never knew who my biological mom was, but I figured out pretty quickly that you were my father."

"How?" Thomas asked.

"As Iris said...." He made a circular gesture at his face. "Hair, bone structure, bushy brows."

They both chuckled.

"Why didn't you tell me you knew?" Thomas asked.

"I like our friendship. I already had a dad, and I didn't need another one." He patted the older man's shoulder. "I like my life, and you've helped teach me so many wonderful things about magic. And you've made me feel sane about my abilities."

"You've always been a bit of a savant when it comes to acquired magic." I heard the pride bursting from him again.

I hated to interrupt, but I was still facing an enemy I couldn't see. "Speaking of acquired magic, can I see the charm bracelet while you finish your happy reunion?"

Father and son. Woo. I couldn't wait to tell Keir that I was right, and he was wrong wrong wrong. As it was, the smile on my face was so big it hurt. "I'm really so happy Carver is okay, and you two are redefining your relationship boundaries." When Carver raised a brow, I added, "My sister Dahlia is a psychologist."

"Ah." Carver nodded. "Got it." He withdrew a yellow satin pouch from his pocket and handed it to me. "Here you go."

I opened the drawstring and dumped the contents into my hand. The eclectic witch had crafted the stones to look like black beads wrapped in gold wire. Marigold's ring was on its side, like a loop, with the gold wire wrapping the band with the peridot looking like a crown of green. The small hag stone Linda had found dangled from the clasp like a charm. There were runes and symbols etched and inlaid with gold on each of the stones. As I turned it in my hands, I could feel the energy pulsing through the elegant piece.

I turned my gaze to Carver. "This is stunning. How did you do this in just a few short hours?"

"With a little help from my friend." He glanced over at Thomas and then back to me.

Thomas nodded. "I managed to tweak Carver's design. It will keep you from being spelled again as long as you're wearing it."

Carver reached out for the bracelet. "Can I put it on you?"

I handed it to him and held out my wrist. "Yes, absolutely." As he laid the bracelet over my skin, his fingertips brushed the hairs on my arm. Fluid energy and power pulsed between us.

"So weird," he said again. He fixed the clasp closed and then looked at Thomas. "My mother was a creature of half air and half water?"

"Yes," the old man confirmed. "She was stunning and powerful. It's no wonder you're exceptional."

I couldn't help but think Carver was taking this more casually than I would've. Hell, I'd spent a couple of days after my magic sparked thinking I had been drugged. "This isn't freaking you out?"

Carver shook his head. "Not yet. But maybe when my edible wears off."

I barked a laugh. "That explains so much. You got any extras?"

"Seriously?" he asked. "Because I do, and I'll give you one."

"Nah," I told him. "I'm good...for now."

"I grew up seeing things that shouldn't exist and feeling things that never made any sense." He shrugged. "The first time I smoked pot, things just made a lot more sense."

"Well, I smoked a little in high school, and while I liked the buzz, I can't say that it gave me any clarity." I giggled. "Just the opposite."

"Do you want me to tell you about your mother?" Thomas asked Carver. "You must have so many questions."

"When the magic took me, I saw everything. It was as if her memories passed through me, and I lived her life, her parents, their parents, and their parents in that short amount of time until Iris touched me." He stared down at me, his smile hesitant. "And then, when I absorbed your tears, I saw your life as well." He turned to Thomas. "I saw your life, too, when I brushed your tears away. You don't have to explain anything. Neither of you. I know what I am. I know who I am." Carver's expression turned solemn. "I am an eclectic witch who also happens to be your water guardian, Iris Everlee."

The door handle rattled, and Keir walked in. He frowned as he glanced at the three of us. "What did I miss?"

"So much," I told him. "So very, very much."

# CHAPTER 15

I HAD BARELY MADE IT THROUGH THE PART OF MY TALE to Keir where Thomas and Carver had shown up when Zev and Marigold strolled into the room.

"I can't believe you had a party and started without me," Marigold said as she handed me the grimoire. "Here's your book. All safe and sound. See, my method is tried and true. No one ever checks under the towel in the backseat."

"Hardy har," I replied. The grimoire warmed as I ran my hand over the cover. "Thank you for bringing it from home. I should've known better than to think I could have a nice vacation away from it for a week."

Zev gave me a bland look. "Was this supposed to be a vacation?"

"It was the first time I've spent a night away from Southill in over four years, so yes," I told him.

"On top of that, it's pretty damn swanky," Marigold added. "If it wasn't for the threat of death, this would be a five-star experience."

"Yeah, the death part really puts a crimp on the whole relaxing week away from home."

I sat down on the bed as the room felt suddenly small with five extra people in it. The hag stone charm on the bracelet clicked against the other stones.

"Ooo," Marigold crooned. "Lemme see it."

I held out my wrist, and my sister came over and examined the piece of jewelry. She ran her fingers over the peridot ring and teared up.

Nope, I thought. None of that. I was just barely holding it together. I took my wrist back from her.

She glanced over her shoulder at Carver. "It's such beautiful workmanship," she told him. "You are a real artist."

Carver gave her a pleased smile. "Thank you."

"How can we test to see if it's working?" Keir asked.

I noticed he and Zev hadn't even looked at each other since the ifrit entered the room. It made me think that the conversation he'd had with Zev had been even more contentious than I'd imagined. I wanted to talk to Keir about it, but the conversation could wait. We had bigger fish to fry, and that was neither a nero nor an ignis joke.

"I'd really like to know as well." I nodded to Carver. "No offense. I'm sure you're very good at what you do."

"None taken. I wouldn't buy a car without kicking the tires first."

"Kicking the tires tells you nothing about a car," Zev said brusquely. At first, I thought it was still about Keir, but then I noticed the way he was noticing the way Carver and Marigold were looking at each other.

Carver gave the ifrit a conciliatory nod. "I'm not opposed to a test drive."

I hoped he was talking about the bracelet and not my sister.

Absently, I traced the symbols on the grimoire. "It's not like I can go around shaking everyone's hand until the stones start to vibrate."

"I'm with Iris on this," Keir agreed. "Besides, I don't want to give Bogmall an inkling that we suspect she's behind the earlier attack. She's smart, and if she thinks we're on to her, she'll pivot."

"Is there anyone here who was close to Bogmall?" Marigold asked. "You know, friends? Family? Lovers? How long was she with the Iron Grove?"

"She transferred here from another grove when she was in her twenties, and she was a part of the Iron Grove for at least twenty years," Keir said. "I remember when she took the job as chief. Freya had offered me the position, but I was working on other stuff." He cast a quick glance at me. "Simon has the job now. He might have more information about her."

"Simon?" At this rate, the guy was never getting off my suspect list. "You think Bogmall and he were close?"

Keir shrugged. "Maybe. Like I said, I never spent much time at the grove. Most of my work for them, much like my father's work, involved travel and diplomacy. And there were a few years I took off for myself."

"To become a puca?" I asked.

Keir smirked. "That, yes, but also the eight years I studied at university to get my doctorate in theology, mythology, and the occult."

"Right," I said. "The ol' college degree." He had taken a sabbatical this semester so that he didn't have to divide his time between work and my disasters. I felt guilty that he was giving up a big part of his life for me.

*Look with your mind, not with your heart. The heart can blind you to what's real.*

I looked around to see who had said those familiar words, then I remembered the woman in the hedge maze. But she hadn't been real, right? Just another hallucination or maybe a vision. She turned into fireflies. Or had she?

"Tell me what's going on in your head?" Keir asked.

"Am I the only one who heard that?"

"Heard what?" Thomas asked.

I guess I was the only one. "There was a woman's voice. She said, look with your mind, not with your heart. The heart can blind you to what's real."

"It sounds like the nonsense your grimoire tells you," Marigold said.

I shook my head and patted the book. "The grim usually has a rhyming scheme."

"Maybe you knocked a screw loose when you hit your head on the dresser earlier," my sister added.

I arched my brow as high as it would go. "This wasn't the first time I heard her."

Thomas, Zev, Carver, and Keir turned their attention to me.

Keir looked confounded and mildly annoyed. "You've been hearing disembodied voices, and you're just now telling me?"

"It wasn't disembodied the last time," I said in my defense. "And it happened after the scary vision of the bearded dudes sacrificing that poor girl. The woman hovered above me while I was down on my back in the grass. She said, *Look with your mind, Iris Everlee, not with your heart. The heart can blind you to what's real.* Then she vanished, and there were fireflies, and then I woke up in bed with a hangover. I don't remember a single thing after that, and until I heard the voice just a minute ago, I'd forgotten all about her."

"What did she look like?" Thomas asked.

"Bronze skin, really bronze, like a statue, and dark curly hair that floated about her head. Oh, and she had dark, golden eyes. And I mean gold the same way that I meant bronze, like metal, only maybe more like a metallic paint because her skin looked incredibly soft." I pivoted my gaze at each one of the men. "Does anyone recognize the description?"

There were a lot of unhelpful shrugs in the room.

Marigold said, "What if she was talking about your grimoire? Maybe she's saying you should look at what it has to say with cold logic and not your emotions."

"Maybe." I doubted it but keeping my emotions in check was always a good idea. I realized then that I'd almost purposefully avoided opening the grimoire. Every time I needed its advice, the damn thing hit me with a rap of doom and gloom. Still, it usually got the solution ball rolling. I lifted my hands. "Fine. I'm asking the grim's advice. Maybe there are enough brains in this room to find some meaning in whatever it has to say."

I sighed. Heavily. "Grim, grim, in my lap. Tell me something good, or get a dirt nap." I grimaced and gave it a gentle pat. "I'm kidding. It's a joke. Don't punish me."

Keir chuckled, then put his hand on my shoulder for emotional support. "You've got this, babe."

I put my hand over his. "Thanks." I steeled my nerves and then opened the giant tome. Signatures with only the year and in different handwriting styles and different inks listed the names of my ancestors.

*Aideen Magee, 1678*

*Clionna Doon, 1705*

*Siobhan Adrian, 1782*

*Mary Ann Langford, 1834*

*Brigit O'Malley, 1880*

*Mira Roberts, 1912*

Below Mira Roberts' name was my signature. I remembered the weight and gravitas I felt when I joined the women of my line in caring for the grimoire and accepting my role as a tru-craft witch.

"What happened between 1912 and now?" Carver asked.

I turned my hand over to show him that I had nothing. "Your guess is as good as mine." As I rested my palms down on the grimoire's pages, I felt the familiar whoosh of energy and adrenaline surge through my veins, and when I picked my hands up, words began to appear on the page on the right.

*Blood of my blood, you must break the ties.*

*Tears of my tears, seek the truth in the lies.*

*A test of skill is a test of will. Do not fail, or it will kill.*

*The waters ahead are uncharted, and the tide won't easily stop once it has started.*

*Goddess, help you.*

BREAKING TIES. With whom? Truth in lies. A big fat, duh. Test of skill leading to death. Tell me something I didn't know. And I was the queen of starting crap I couldn't stop. None of this seemed like new information. I slapped the cover shut and stifled a frustrated scream. "Clear as a fudge sundae and about as helpful as a kick in the head."

A frantic tapping at the window was the only thing that snapped me out of my reverie. We all looked over and saw Fair Konig slapping at the windowpane with his wings and his sword.

"What the hell?" I asked.

Keir beat everyone to the window, and he unlatched the frame and slid it up. The pixie king sliced through the screen and dove inside the room. He was panting, and his face was apple-red.

"Linda!" he shouted, his voice jumping up an octave higher than normal as he gasped for air. "It's Li...Linda! She's in trouble."

I set the grim aside and jumped to my feet as fear for my gnome sent my pulse racing. "Where's Linda? What kind of trouble?"

"A snotgurgle," he said.

"A what?" I asked, completely appalled.

"It sounded like he said snotgurgle," my sister replied. "What's a snotgurgle?"

I wasn't sure I wanted to know, but this was Linda's life we were talking about, so I would stuff my repulsion down for now.

Keir said, "A snotgurgle is a rare kind of troll that takes great delight in torturing its food before eating it. Gnomes are one of its favorites."

"Why would someone give it such a gross name?" Carver asked.

"Because it produces a lot of mucus and phlegm like digestive juices and saliva that helps it to break down the stone structure that gnomes are made from."

"Oh, my god!" My mouth dropped open, but I closed it when my stomach lurched. "We're not letting that happen to Linda." I pointed at the door. "Everyone out, so I can get dressed. We're going troll hunting."

# CHAPTER 16

When I heard the term snotgurgle, it conjured up some of the most disgusting, little green, slime-driven creatures I could imagine. It turned out I had a very limited imagination. The beast stood seven feet tall with yellow waxy skin that oozed green pus from boils and sores that covered most of his exposed body. His nose took up the majority of real estate on his face. It was shaped like an ornamental gourd that was skinny and curved at the top, fat and bulbous at the end and covered in lumpy-bumpies. Only this gourd oozed chartreuse mucous from a single hole in the tip.

"*Lass mich runter, dreckiges Biest,*" Linda screeched as the troll-kin dangled her from one leg. Linda's hat was on the ground at its feet, broken into several pieces, and her right hand was missing.

Keir, Zev, and I hid in the dense underbrush, waiting for a moment to take the foul creature by surprise. "That son-of-a-bitch," I hissed as I lurched forward. Zev and Keir tugged me back into hiding.

The snotgurgle chortled a high-pitched trill as it danced around a large boulder near a shallow stream at the end of the property. The stench, like untreated raw sewage, made me gag. Thanks to my puking adventures earlier, there were no cookies left inside me to toss.

Instead, I was filled with pure, unadulterated rage that made me want to turn the creature's bones to dust, set its ass on fire, and suffocate it by removing all the air from its lungs, but Keir had informed me that snotgurgles were immune to magic. Hell, due to the properties of the mucous that covered their bodies from head to toe, they were immune to most physical attacks. On top of that, the mucous was poisonous to humans and many humanoid creatures, and the snot from its nose could burn through the skin like flesh-dissolving hydrochloric acid.

All this meant that a direct assault was likely to end with all of us dead except Zev. The djinn was immortal. However, it could still do some major damage to him.

Thomas, Carver, and Marigold stayed behind to alert the Iron Grove security team to a troll invasion. According to Thomas, something must have gone seriously wrong with the wards surrounding the compound. A snotgurgle shouldn't have been able to come within a mile of the boundaries without it setting off warning alarms.

Keir had been concerned with how a snotgurgle ended up in Michigan in the first place. They were not only rare in general, but he'd also never heard of one living in the United States. Snotgurgles were Scandinavian in origin. Someone had to have assisted the troll-kin to cross the ocean.

At the moment, I didn't care how it had gotten to the Iron Grove compound. I only cared that it had Linda.

I summoned my power and focused my energy on the snotgurgles wiry hair dome. "Bone beneath the skin of this ugly troll-kin, break and shake, for Linda's sake," I incanted.

The snotgurgle sneezed, and fluorescent green globs shot from the hole in its nose and landed on a nearby tree. The goozy gunk burned a giant hole in the tree bark. He trilled with laughter again, then threw Linda in the air.

"*Scheisse!*" she screamed.

It caught her and danced again. "*Baka, baka liten kaka, rulla, rulla liten bulla!*" the snotgurgle sang.

"What is it saying?" I asked.

Fair Konig buzzed into my ear. "Bake, bake, little cake. Roll, roll, little bun. It's a Swedish children's nursery rhyme to lull children to sleep. It is similar to our *Backe, backe Kuchen*, and your Patty-cake song." He shook his sword in the air. "He is going to eat her. We must do something." His angry wings clipped my cheek.

I jerked away. "Ouch."

"I apologize, but I can't do nothing."

The troll threw Linda up in the air again, and her curses were only half-hearted. Oh, no. She was losing hope. I had an idea. Probably not a good one, but like the pixie king, I couldn't keep hiding in the bushes and do nothing. I spoke in hushed tones. "Can you grab Linda the next time he throws her in the air?"

He frowned, his expression helpless. "She's too heavy for me to carry, or I would have flown her out when he first made a grab for her. I barely escaped the poor tree's fate."

The tree that had been hit by super snot was starting to rapidly decay to its core. "Well, poop." Then I got another bad idea. "Can you just knock her away? Just give her a hearty shove so that she lands out of his reach. That will give her a chance to dig her way to safety."

Keir put his hand on my arm and shook his head. "She is fully slimed. Her own magic won't work on her. Even if Fair Konig manages to knock her a few feet away, she won't be able to escape."

I stifled a frustrated groan. *Damn it*! If she was coated in anti-magic mucus, then there wasn't any spell I could perform that would help her, either. This couldn't be the end of Linda. I wouldn't allow it. I'd faced a world-destroying god and defeated him. I could take on one boogery butthead who tortured and ate gnomes for fun.

"Iris...." I heard an edge to Keir's voice as if he was worried that I was planning something reckless and not well thought out.

He knew me so well. I sprinted forward, kicking at Zev's hand when he tried to grab my leg. "Hey, snot bucket!" I yelled. "Pick on someone a little closer to your size!"

His head snapped up, and a slimy rocket shot from his nostril. Keir, in full homicidal bunny mode, knocked me sideways to protect me from getting hit. I rolled on my shoulder, like Luanne had taught me, and came up onto my feet in a crouch.

The snotgurgle had a real belly laugh as he assessed our threat level. "*Mjuka smörkakor, mums mums.*" He smacked his lips and patted his stomach with his free hand. He sounded scarily similar to the Swedish chef from the *Muppet Show*.

"He says, soft butter cakes, yum, yum," Fair Konig squeaked. "He wants to eat you too now!"

Even without the translation, I'd gotten the gist. "Well, he's going to have to go hungry tonight because this asswipe isn't eating anyone."

"No, *Leibling!*" Linda chided. "Run."

Keir and I stood several feet apart, facing one of the most disgusting, vile enemies I'd ever had the misfortune to meet, and Zev was nowhere to be seen. Had the ifrit deserted us? I knew his self-preservation instinct was strong, and he'd been angry about Keir ordering him to the grove, but damn, this was a cold move. I'd really thought we were at least friends.

The snotgurgle shook Linda by the leg. Now that we were closer, the slime that coated her glistened in the moonlight. Keir had said that tomorrow would be the Harvest moon. Its energy would amplify my powers. I wondered if that's why I'd managed to trigger nero-craft. It also gave me another less stupid idea. At least, I hoped it was less stupid.

I glanced at Keir, and he met my gaze with his dark, tarry Puca orbs. "Can you keep him busy for a minute?" I asked.

He nodded. "Yes." He bared his sharp teeth and clicked his black diamond claws. "Whatever you're planning, make it fast."

"I will," I promised, hoping I wasn't lying. "Don't die."

His ears twitched back and forth on top of his black furry head. "I won't if you won't."

"Deal."

Keir leaped over the top of the snotgurgle's head, and I prayed to all the gods I could think of, and some of the ones I couldn't, that my plan had a shot in hell of working.

I focused my energy on the small stream behind the troll-kin. Trying to tap into my nero-craft, I reached out to the water, beckoning it to heed my call. *Please work*, I silently pleaded.

I went with the first rhyme I could think of, *The Rime of the Ancient Mariner*, and changed it to suit my needs, "*Water, water everywhere, and not a drop to drink. The very beast does rot my gnome, and this should never be. Let the slimy thing get purged and cleaned, and let the magic see.*" The spell was sloppy, but I held my intention clear and firm in my head. I let out a noise of frustration when the water from the stream failed to bend to my will. What was I doing wrong? I was open to the magic. There wasn't a single thing inside me resisting it. *Come on, nero-craft*, I cajoled. *Don't let me down.*

Keir was circling the snotgurgle at warp speed, and snot bombs were dropping all over the perimeter, but I was relieved to see that my guy was dodging them like a champ. In the race between the snotgurgle and the hare, the hare was winning.

He was doing his part. It was time to do mine. I dug my fingernails into my palm until I broke through my skin, and I started to bleed.

"Blood of my blood," I said, borrowing the line from my grimoire. "Let the motherfucking tide flow." I flung my bleeding hand toward the creek. "*Water, water, every-*

*where, stop messing with my chi. Douse the gnome and bring her home.*" When it didn't react again. I shouted, "I can't do this without her." I squeezed my hand into a fist. "Wash her body of slime and snot, do this now before she does rot."

I let out a cry of anger and grief as the water refused to do anything I wanted. "Damn it all to hell!" Just once, could my magic work the way it was supposed to freaking work?

The moonlight dimmed, and Fair Konig shouted, "Look out!"

I whipped my gaze to the sky, fully expecting a snot missile of death. Instead, a massive bubble of green hung directly over our heads, effectively blocking the moon. "What the—?"

The bubble popped. Thousands of gallons of water rained down on us like it was monsoon season.

"Oh, shiiiiiiiiiiite!" I hollered as the water smashed me against the ground and brought with it a hail of foot-long fishes. I shut up quick when I swallowed a mouthful of the murky liquid. My Puca scooped me up as the water washed down into the creek and away from the area. The snotgurgle was face down on the ground, getting tail-slapped by struggling bass trying to make their way to the creek, and it was starting to move.

"Linda," I grunted. "Where's Linda?"

"Over here!" Fair Konig alerted. The gnome was picking through the pieces of her broken hat.

"Leave it," I told her. "Go, get underground."

Her pale bald head was once again bathed in moon-light. "Not without my hand."

"Life now," I told her. "Hand later. Go!"

The snotgurgle was getting to his feet.

"Go!" I ordered. "Now."

Linda turned her back and vanished through the ground.

I let out a quick breath. It worked. Washing the goop off Linda had made using her magic possible again and saved her life. Of course, the shallow stream was more like a small river now. Where in the heck had all that water come from?

# CHAPTER 17

THE WOODS AT THE NORTH END OF THE COMPOUND HAD a dense underbrush that kept me from going as fast as I wanted. Even with my newly acquired fitness regimen, I couldn't seem to get my knees up high enough to jump over fallen logs, brightly colored poison ivy thickets, fragrant sumac bushes, and an ungodly number of naked twigs that switched my legs with every stride. Add in wet clothes, and it made running away a nightmare.

However, when a snotgurgle is chasing your tail, you do everything in your power to haul ass. So, haul ass, I did.

Thankfully, snotgurgles run about as fast as a five-year-old. Slower than us but relentlessly steady. We managed to put a little distance between us and the creature, but not enough to stop.

Keir moderated his pace to fit mine as Fair Konig led us through the trees to the compound's boundaries. Even so, I had no idea what we were going to do once we got there. It would be irresponsible to unleash the brutal booger machine on civilians. We had to figure out a way to contain and kill the evil bastard before it killed us or anyone else.

"What's the plan?" I yelled to Keir. "We can't just—" I didn't finish the sentence as the tip of my toe caught on a vine that stuck up from the ground. I lifted my foot, thinking I could recover my balance, but the tip of my sneaker caught on a sharp edge and sent me careening forward. I smacked the ground harder than I thought possible. My left knee, right hip, and both palms took the brunt of the impact. The jarring pain knocked the breath right out of me.

"Son of a bitch!" I wheezed.

I could hear the snotgurgle in the distance, laughing with glee. The beast had wicked good hearing.

"Watch your footing, *sahira*," Zev said unhelpfully as he appeared beside me.

I wanted to yell, "Where the hell have you been?" but I was still having trouble formulating words through the pain.

Fair Konig frantically zipped back and forth above me, his wings moving so fast they created a droning hum. "Hurry," he insisted. "He's not far behind us."

As if I'd planned to slow our pace and give myself whiplash in the process...

Keir knelt beside me. "Can you walk, or do you want me to carry you?"

"I can take her away from here and then return," Zev suggested.

"No," I rejected his offer. I wouldn't leave Keir and the pixie king to deal with the snotgurgle. Zev said he'd return, but after the way he'd taken off and deserted us earlier, I didn't trust him. "Give me a second." I was still trying to assess how much damage I'd done to my body.

*Did my legs still work? Yes. Did my arms still move? Yes.*

I nodded to Keir. "If you help me up, I can run."

"Deal." He took my hands and lifted me to my feet.

"Hurry," Fair Konig shrieked. "He's coming."

"I'm hurrying," I told him as I brushed off my knee and bent it to make sure I could. Then I took off in a jog.

Keir took up the position to my left and Zev to my right. "Where is Linda?" the ifrit asked.

"Like you care," I spat back. "You left us. Why would you do that?" I waved off any excuse he might have. I understood being afraid, but in my book, his move had put him in the coward category. Even so, he'd come back. I wanted to let that count for something, but I was struggling to figure out how. "It doesn't matter now. We might not be able to kill it, but we need to find a way to contain this monster."

Zev suddenly stopped. He turned around and yelled, "Here, *alwahsh alnajis!*" He was waving his arms like a madman. The troll-kin roared as it burst through the trees. Zev took off on a path away from us.

"What's he doing?" I asked Keir.

The black had drained from his eyes as he stared at the fleeing djinn in disbelief. "He's leading it toward the mansion."

My heart sank at his words. I shook my head.

Marigold was at the mansion, and she didn't always think about consequences when throwing herself in the path of danger. With this creature, the only outcome was rotting death. "We have to stop him." I didn't wait for Keir to reply as I pivoted his direction and ran after Zev and the snotgurgle.

THE MEGA-MANSION WAS LIT up just beyond the break in the woods. Keir, who had raced ahead of me, stopped abruptly as we saw a line of people stretched out along the border of the hedge maze from one end to the other. A wall of defense between the snotgurgle and the compound.

It looked as if the groups were sectioned by groves. I recognized the archdruids Freya, Mathias Easter of Bezoar, Derrick Asher of Green, Jerriah Dale of Mountain Ash, Telva Mack of Luna, and Yasmine Leafborne of Shining River. Each archdruid stood in front of their people, along with what I assumed were their coven leaders.

Freya stood with Thomas, and the others each had a man or a woman by their side. They joined hands.

I pointed at the snotgurgle. "And what in the hell is it doing?"

The creature had stopped in the middle of the field and began doing a series of awkwardly uncoordinated flips, spins, kicks, and cartwheels. It was like watching a drunken circus monkey. Even more horrifying, mucus spritzed from his body boils like particles from a hard sneeze. Only this spray of terror was continuous.

"The beast is putting on a display of his prowess to frighten his enemies," Keir told me. "I've read about it, but seeing it is just...."

"Disgusting," I finished for him. "What about the archdruids?"

"They are joining their covens through the ties between the archdruids." He sounded awed. "I've only ever heard about this ritual. I've never seen it in practice, and for good reason. It's a temporary binding spell that creates a bond to share elemental magic between the factions. It creates a kind of magic that is unmatched in the supernatural world." I could see the concern in the grim set of his mouth.

"But?" I asked because there is always a *but*.

"But," Keir went on. "While it makes every druid and tru-craft witch exponentially more powerful while they are working as the group, it also makes them more vulnerable to attacks from anyone inside the spell who wants to take advantage of a weakness. It can be seriously dangerous for those doing the ritual in good faith if some dick decides to make a power grab during the ritual."

"That is a downside," I agreed. "Even so, what good does bigger magic do if the snotgurgle is immune to magic." Well, its snot was, anyhow. But since the creature was dripping with the stuff, it amounted to the same thing. "What can they do?"

He turned his worried gaze to mine. "I don't know, but Freya is an expert in the mythologies of monsters. The troll-kin must have a weakness that I'm not aware of. I'm sure she has a plan."

He didn't sound convinced.

"I hope you're right."

The snotgurgle was less than impressed by the display of foes as he continued to perform the uncoordinated dance of death. The full moon made his horrifying gyrations even more surreal.

"Power of air," Thomas intoned. "I bind thee to mine and thine, my kin to call and summon. Obey my will." I waited for a gust or wall of wind, but nothing happened. I didn't get it. Was his tru-craft failing? Was the snotgurgle somehow blocking his ability?

"Power of fire," a tall brunette with straight dark hair, close to Yasmine Leafborne, said, "I bind thee to mine and thine, my kin to call and summon. Obey my will."

"Power of earth," said a plump woman wearing a bright red rockabilly dress covered in white polka dots and standing beside to Derrick Asher, "I bind thee to mine and thine, my kin to call and summon. Obey my will."

Still, there was nothing in the air that I could detect magic-wise. We were doomed.

A petite blonde in a long white maxi dress, with Telva Mack, spoke. "Power of water, I bind thee to mine and thine, my kin to call and summon. Obey my will."

That was four elements from four out of the six groves.

Mountain Ash was next. A woman with dark hair and serious curves moved over near Jerriah Dale and said,

"Power of Air, I bind thee to mine and thine, my kin to call and summon. Obey my will."

That left only the Bezoar Grove to join in, and I wondered if Mathias Easton, the Ichabod Crane-looking leader of the grove, would allow old scars to see this assault on Iron Grove as an opportunity.

Easton's coven leader, a guy who was just as skinny and tall as he was, after only a moment of hesitation, added his own command. "Power of Fire, I bind thee to mine and thine, my kin to call and summon. Obey my will."

I waited. Again, nothing happened. Even the snot-gurgle seemed confused.

"Am I missing something?" I asked Keir.

He shrugged. "I don't think so."

"Then why isn't anything happening?"

Before Keir could answer me, there was a sonic boom that struck the center of the field as all the druids and witches joined hands. The force of it blew me off my feet, and Keir caught me mid-air and rolled us away out of the path as another blow shook the ground beneath us.

I was on top of him, panting as the adrenaline surge made my heart flutter and shortened my breaths. "What the unholy hell was that?"

"Explosion magic," Keir said. "They're trying to blow it up."

The snotgurgle trilled with wicked joviality as it danced around inside the crater that had formed, then in a move that I thought impossible from the clumsy oaf, it leaped ten feet into the air and onto the grass in front of the hole the witches had made.

"It didn't work."

Keir gave me a "duh" look but had the good sense not to say it.

There was a collective gasp from the grove groups, then a lot of running as the snotgurgle rapid-fired snot loads at the druids and witches.

"I can't watch this from the sidelines." Especially since I knew my sister was on the other side of the line. If the snotgurgle got past the groves, there would be nothing stopping it from going on a homicidal rampage through the Iron Grove compound. "We can't let it get to the mansion."

"I'm not sure how to stop it. Leading it away was the best option," Keir said.

"What if I join my power with the groves?" I asked. "I'm strong. You've told me yourself that I have more magic than anyone has seen in a long time. I can make the groves and their covens stronger. Could that work?"

Keir was shaking his head. "No. I can't...I won't. Iris, don't do this. You're already under attack from someone here at the grove. Binding your power to theirs, even for a short period of time, is as dangerous as it is stupid. If Bogmall is in that line, she will swallow you whole and never spit you out."

The thought of making myself even more vulnerable to an attack from the blonde bitch made my head swim. "You're right," I told him. "It's too dangerous." But so was doing nothing.

And then the worst possible scenario happened. Zev jumped in front of Freya to take a snot-rocket hit, and I heard a familiar cry of anguish as my sister Marigold ran out from behind a hedge and toward the field of battle.

"No!" I cried out. "Go back!" What was my sister thinking?

Luanne stepped out of the groves' line of defense, and she was running to cut Marigold off before my sister could get in range of the creature's acid spray.

She wasn't going to make it. Marigold sprinted, her maxiskirt hiked up to her knees like a woman possessed.

Keir's skin split wide, and coarse black fur replaced it as his puca form burst from inside him. He could adjust his size and height in this incarnation, and he made himself at least eight feet tall. "I will protect her," he said before moving inhumanly fast toward the foray.

But who would protect him? Zev was a powerful djinn, and he hadn't gotten off the ground since the rotting slime had hit him in the chest.

Luanne was down now, and Corina, the water witch, was spraying her down.

Marigold was almost to the field. Druids and witches were falling like dominoes. Bogmall, be damned, I couldn't let the people I loved and cared about suffer because I was too afraid to fight with them. What I really needed was something more powerful than me. More powerful than all of us.

I lifted my voice to the sky, begging the near Harvest moon for any help it could give, and said, "Power of earth, fire, air, and water, I bind thee to mine and thine, my kin to call and summon. Obey my will."

The second the words left my lips, I felt a shock as if every nerve in my body was suddenly electrified, and my skin began to glow green, red, blue, and yellow. My skin burned, pulled, and tightened as if it was trying to escape my body. I didn't blame it. I was ready to escape as well.

Without any will of my own, I floated ten feet into the air and flew just above the snotgurgle.

"Iris!" Keir roared. "Don't—"

My mouth opened, and a voice that was not my own said, "I am Macha, earth mother and destroyer of men. You will come to heel!"

# CHAPTER 18

SEVERAL OF THE WITCHES AND MOST OF THE DRUIDS dropped to the ground as light beams flew off my skin, washing the decimated field with energy that crippled my brain. I'd had a fire god threaten to use me as a meat suit but hearing about it and having it happen were two very different experiences.

The snotgurgle bellowed, beating its chest with its hammy fists as its flesh-rotting sputum doubled the ooze to coat his body in protection.

Macha turned her gaze below. "Addlebyörn Bulbusbil-gerbiersven of Höga Kusten."

The troll-kin looked up in surprise. "*Du vet mitt namn?*"

My brain translated the sentence to, "you know my name?"

It shot a hot glob at us, and Macha used our hand to swat away the gunk. The light that bathed our skin nulli-fied the corrosive properties. She set us down on the ground in front of the snotgurgle. "You cannot defeat me, creature," she told it. "I am your undoing."

His words were foreign, but Macha translated them once again. "I do not bow to you, pretender. You are no god of mine."

"Poor creature." Her voice softened. "Let me show you how very wrong you are."

My mind screamed for her to stop as she reached out with my hand and laid it on the snotgurgle's smarmy skin. A boil popped under my palm, and I reeled with revulsion. Still, Macha held us firmly in place.

"Be transformed, Addlebyörn Bulbusbilgerbiersven of Höga Kusten." Our hands glowed with such intensity it made our eyes water. The snotgurgles beady eyes widened to the size of silver dollars as, one by one, the pustules on his skin closed and shriveled.

"Noooooo!" it thundered. It tried to yank its body away from us, but Macha's awe-inspiring power held it firmly in place.

As the boils disappeared, the snotgurgles skin turned gray, and it began to grow shorter and thinner. Even its nose changed shape to something wider, flatter, and with two nostrils instead of one. The creature shrieked, its voice pitching up an octave as it shrank to only a foot tall, and it grew a long white beard. I was surprised when I realized it now bore a striking resemblance to a gnome.

"Now, *Nisse* Addlebyörn, go and be at peace," we told it. "If you can find it." I knew from her thoughts that a Nisse was a small creature very similar to gnomes, and I thought its new form was fitting. We flicked the ex-snotgurgle, and he went flying until we could no longer see him.

"Iris!" someone yelled.

Macha turned our head. It was Keir, no longer in his puca form, and he was kneeling next to Zev and someone else. My mind was on fire, and it was so hard to concentrate.

Then, through Macha's eyes, I saw the scene so clearly. There was a woman with dark hair in a flowy skirt on the ground next to Zev. Acid from the snotgurgle was burning through her side, and some had splattered her face. Keir's face was shot through with anguish. The ifrit, his own chest rotting through, crawled to the woman and pulled her into his arms. He cradled her as he cried flames down his cheeks.

No, I thought to Macha. No. It wasn't just a woman. It wasn't just a...Marigold. The thought finally broke through. It was Marigold. Oh, goddess. A knot of fear gripped my throat. *Save her*, I demanded.

"We can't save what she is," Macha said.

*You just turned a ten-foot slime-covered beast into a tiny benign creature. You can save her.*

"There is a cost...."

"We're losing her!" Keir shouted. "Iris!"

*I'll pay the price*, I told her. *Whatever you want. Save my sister.*

She walked us to where Zev held Marigold, his grief palpable as he faced mortality.

"The rot is making it impossible to heal her," Keir said. "We can't stop it. Every time Zev tries, it takes more from her. It takes more from him. It's like it's feeding on the magic."

We squatted next to the pitiful, dying creatures.

*Not pitiful,* I thought, forcing Macha's opinion away. These were two people I cared about. I loved. My sister was my best friend, my rock, and I would do anything to make this right.

"Anything has a broad scope, child," Macha said. "Do not negotiate with your heart."

This wasn't a negotiation. This was a hostage situation, and I was at the mercy of my hijacker.

Macha chuckled. "Humans are such fascinating creatures."

"Iris," Keir said. "What is going on? Where are you?"

*I'm here*, I thought. I need Macha for a while longer. Long enough to fix Marigold.

"I will *fix* the woman, as you say, Iris Everlee," Macha said. I registered the surprise in the goddess's head when she laid our hands on Marigold's cold arm. "Oh. I didn't realize." For whatever reason, she shut me out of her thoughts then.

*Macha?* When she didn't answer, I screamed, *Macha!*

Finally, she said, "Olwen, who faced thirteen harrowing trials to win the heart of her love. Your line runs true in this one. She is strong. A warrior's heart." Our hands glowed as they had when Macha changed the snotgurgle. "Transform, daughter," Macha said. "Transform and live."

I prayed my sister didn't turn into a one-foot bearded Nisse, but I would have taken it if that was the only way to keep her alive. I watched as her rotting flesh began to fill in with newly formed bone, muscle, and skin. The pits in her face where she'd been splattered healed to a radiant, smooth finish.

Zev let out a heaving sigh as the rise and fall of her chest grew stronger, and he let her go when it was apparent she would live. He let her go and fell over, and the fire in his eyes had died out.

Macha touched his face. "Your time is not over, Za'fir of Mesopotamia. This is just the first trial on your path to love." Our hand glowed again as we bathed the djinn in light. "Transform and live. Live to fulfill your path."

Zev's chest closed up, and his eyes shot open. He opened his mouth, and a fire emptied fifteen feet into the sky, and when the flames finally went out, he collapsed back and passed out.

I felt Macha smile. "I have done as you've asked. Now it's your turn to know the cost."

My stomach twisted. I'd agreed to do anything the goddess wanted.

"When I am in need, you will be my sword, my shield, and my vessel. Until then, you may live your life as you see fit."

*And if I die before then?* After all, the possibility of dying was an almost daily occurrence. But I was curious as to how she would exact her payment if I wasn't around to collect.

"If you die before I have need of you, everything I have done will be undone. Including your sister's life." Ominously, she added, "Living is the better option. Figure out a way to survive what's coming next."

"What's coming next?" I asked, but there was no

response. My skin felt cold, but I could breathe again, and I could think again, and I was once again in control of my body.

Keir, who'd been watching the exchange between the goddess and me, lifted his brow. "Iris?"

I nodded as my legs went wobbly, and I fell forward. Keir caught me in his arms. He brushed my hair back from my face, his eyes pinched with worry.

"I'm here," I told him. "She's gone."

I felt his relief as he gathered me in his arms and he buried my face in his neck. "You scared the shit out of me."

"I'm sorry." I wrapped my arms around his neck. I held him like my life depended on it. "Marigold?"

"She's breathing. I think she's going to be okay. Zev too."

"Thank God." In this case, it was *goddess*, but I was hesitant to invoke her again with any intention.

Keir helped me to my feet as druids with stretchers, including Simon, Harry, and Hellie hauled the wounded from the field. When they came for Marigold and Zev, they tried to get me on one as well.

Keir waved them away as he lifted me into his arms. "I've got her," he said to Harry when the druid tried to collect me.

My heart contracted with guilt as I remembered Luanne running to intercept my sister. "Where's Lu?"

Harry said, "She took a bad hit to the arm, but the water witch was able to get the poison washed off her skin before it got into her bloodstream and took hold. She got lucky." He gave me a quick nod. "Thanks to you, we all got lucky. This could've turned out so much worse."

Again, it wasn't thanks to me. I'd had nothing to do with the takedown of the snotgurgle. I'd merely opened myself up for possession, and a goddess took it as an invitation. I shivered. Keir had been right about the binding making me vulnerable. If it had been a malevolent god or Bogmall who had taken control of my body, the outcome could've been devastating.

"I'm going to need at least four hot showers to wash this day away." I clung to Keir as he jogged toward the mansion. "That was so much worse than anything I've ever faced. And Linda...." My heart sank for my gnome mentor. "We have to find her. She needs me."

"We'll find her." Keir kissed my forehead. "Thanks to you, she's alive. Thanks to you, all of us are alive."

"It was foolish," I told him. "And reckless." Even so, I knew in my heart I'd have done it again under the same circumstances.

"Agreed," he said. "Foolish and reckless, but also brave and wonderful."

"Make sure that's what they write on my headstone." I cracked a smile so he knew I was only half serious.

We were stopped just outside the mansion by Freya, Derrick Asher, Telva Mack and Jerriah Dale. Their tru-craft witches were with them.

"Thank you, Iris," Freya said. "This night could've ended much differently."

"I didn't do anything," I told her. "It was Macha, the creator goddess. She won the fight for us tonight."

Freya's gaze darkened. "We still give thanks."

Telva Mack nodded. "I thought it was such. Your witch stumbled into our spell and opened us all up to the wrath of a god. What if she had invoked someone like Draugr, Loviator, or the Morigu? They would have possessed us all, and no one would've survived."

"But she didn't," Thomas snapped. "Iris's quick action and willingness to sacrifice herself for others is the only reason any of us are here."

I moved to get out of Keir's arms, and he set me down. I gave Thomas a grateful smile. "The Luna Grove archdruid is right. I stepped into it tonight without thinking. I'm glad my actions got rid of the snotgurgle, but I recognized that it could have been different had it not been for Macha."

"You're being too hard on yourself," Derrick said. He gave Telva Mack a stern glare. "And you're being ungrateful. I think Iris more than proved her power tonight."

Jerriah nodded. "I agree. Iris Everlee is an asset to the groves."

Mathias Easton joined us. "We shall see when she is tested tomorrow night."

"You have got to be kidding me," Keir ground out. "You had to have felt all her elements. To test her now is pomp and circumstance. It's just you peacocking your own power."

"Keir," Freya warned. "Take a step back."

"No," he challenged her. "Not where Iris is concerned. I won't let you all turn this into a witch hunt."

Derrick cleared his throat. "I'm sorry, Keir. I know this isn't what you want to hear, but Iris still needs to show us she can control the elements she claims as part of her tru-craft. It's not personal. She saved the groves tonight, but on the other hand, she emptied an entire pond from a mile away."

"I did what?"

"The water you used to douse the troll-kin, it was from a stock pond at a hatchery down the road," the water witch Corina said. "You moved it a mile to drop it onto the creature."

I blinked. "I was trying to pull from the stream...."

The blonde woman nodded. "Your power sought out the largest water mass it could find. What if it had been Lake Superior? Instead of forty thousand gallons of pond water, you might have unloaded hundreds of thousands of lake water into the area. Drowning everything for miles. Your control is suspect, and that's why the trials need to happen."

Keir's body was rigid next to mine. I could tell it was taking all his effort not to unleash holy puca hell on their asses. I grabbed his hands and laced my fingers with his.

"I've got this," I said quietly for his sake. "I accept," I told the druids and the witches. "I'll take your tests, and when I pass them, I expect that you will never talk of binding my magic again." I'd felt their power tonight, the same as they had felt mine, and I knew one important thing that they didn't, I was going to win. There wasn't any other choice.

Keir put his arm around me as druids and coven members alike who had been helping the wounded gathered at the entrance. They clapped for me as Keir walked me past them, gauntlet-style.

Carver met us at the top of the steps. "Nice save." His

smile was wistful as he moved aside. "I could feel the pull on my element when you worked your nero-craft. It's going to be interesting being your guardian."

"If I survive tomorrow," I joked.

Keir didn't think it was funny.

Before we got to the stairs, I felt a buzzing sensation on my wrist. I looked down, and the hag stone on the charm was glowing, and the stones were getting warm against my skin. "Spirit magic," I hissed. "Someone is casting a spell."

Keir and I whipped around to face the crowd of familiar and unfamiliar faces as we scanned the room for anyone that screamed, *hey, it's me, Bogmall*.

Instead, we were met with more claps and cheers of goodwill. The vibration grew more intense. I wrapped my other hand around my wrist. "We have to go," I told Keir. "We have to go now."

# CHAPTER 19

THE FURTHER UP THE STAIRS WE GOT, THE LESS INTENSE the vibration on the bracelet, and when we reached the second floor, it was completely gone. Whoever had been channeling anima hadn't followed us. The goal of having the charm was to have a secret early warning system to find the person who might be possessed by Bogmall. The way I'd grabbed the bracelet and ran might've given the sorcerer a clue that I was on to her dickhead ways. Ugh.

"I didn't play that cool at all," I said to Keir as we strolled down the hall. My legs didn't feel like gelatin anymore, and I took some pride in the fact that I was managing to stay upright.

He shook his head. "I wish there hadn't been half the compound in the foyer. The suspect pool is huge."

Why couldn't this bitch just let it go? Would I be satisfied when she was eventually hunted down and strung up by her thumbs? Absolutely. But I wasn't going to do the tracking myself. Her obsession with me was putting her in the path of danger as well. I couldn't understand it.

If she could take out an anima-craft witch, why did she need the other elements? The answer was she didn't. However, she wanted my power all the same. Which meant I wasn't safe, a given, but it also meant my sister wasn't safe, and neither was Keir, Luanne, and anyone else I cared about, including my guardians, Linda, Zev, Fair Konig, and now Carver.

Was that the reason the snotgurgle had been released on the compound? Had the hexen-bitch used the disgusting creature as a way to get to Linda? As a way to force me to use my magic to an extreme where it might burn me to dust? If it had been her strategy, it had been a good one. It had nearly worked.

"I need to check on my sister and your sister, and Zev, of course." I was still a little angry that he'd deserted us when Linda's life was on the line. Since he'd nearly died, and my sister nearly died trying to save him, I decided to wait until he was healthy before I throttled him. "Where do you think they took her? And I want to find Linda. She was so distraught when she'd been forced to flee. I've never seen her so...broken." Literally and figuratively.

When I'd accidentally brought Fair Konig into our lives, Linda and he shared a history that had brought up old wounds for her. While she'd been angry and hurt that I wouldn't send the pixies away, she'd retained a feisty quality that defined her as a gnome. Tonight, she had pieces of her ripped away and other pieces dissolved. I didn't know if she would ever be whole again. Even so, I was going to do everything in my power to make sure she got back some of what she lost.

I had to find her first.

Keir stopped mid-stride. "They're probably using the ballroom on the first floor as a makeshift hospital. There were a lot of wounded, and that's the biggest empty space the mansion has available. Do you want to go now or after a shower?"

It was a no-brainer. "Sisters first, shower later." I had to see for myself that they were both alive and well.

THE BALLROOM SMELLED of medicinal herbs, alkaloids, and snotgurgle stench. When the goddess had taken me, the smell had faded, but now that I was in a room where the clothes of the fallen had been cut up and piled into heavy plastic waste bins, the stench was back.

I pressed my fingers to my lips.

"Someone needs to get those rags out of here," Keir commanded. "Now." He might not hold rank, but he had a gravitas to him that no one argued with. Besides, I was pretty sure the entire place saw him go full vampire-bunny-alope when he jumped into the fray. No one was going to challenge him. Not if they knew what was good for them.

Hellie, who'd been tending to Luanne on the far side of the room, volunteered. "I'll get it." She rushed to the first bin and pushed it out of the back door.

Luanne was sitting up on a cot, drinking a juice box. She waved at us. That simple gesture took the steam right out of my badass puca. I leaned my shoulder against his. "Go. Go see your sister."

I looked around. "I'm going to find mine."

Keir nodded, and our paths diverged. I didn't see Marigold on any of the recovery cots, but I hadn't checked behind the curtains where they were keeping the more seriously wounded. The first one I checked had a familiar white-haired man who had been one of my main suspects...until now. My charm bracelet was cold and still. Simon, who was unconscious, had a major chunk of his right thigh missing. It looked as if someone had gone in with a carving knife and cut his muscle out to the bone.

"Oh, god," I whispered. It was awful. Thomas came up behind me. "We had to cut all the necrotizing tissue out of the wound," he said. "He'll recover, but he'll never have the same strength in that leg, and I'm afraid he'll always have pain." The old man rubbed his weary eyes. "Still, he'll live, and that's something to be thankful for."

"This is my fault," I said.

"You didn't set a toxic troll on us, Iris. You can't take the blame for something beyond your control."

"If Bogmall wasn't after me, everyone would be safe."

Thomas shook his head. "For an intelligent, capable young woman, you can be dense sometimes."

My gaze flicked to his. "Are you trying to tell me I'm thick-headed?"

"Are you trying to tell me that you would've preferred for Bogmall to kill you in your first encounter with her? Because I don't understand what you think you could've done, other than die, to prevent any of this. You were born to tru-craft. You didn't seek it."

"Yeah, but I just kept pushing my luck with my grimoire and kept triggering different elements. I should've stopped at earth."

"Like the sun can stop the moon from rising?" he asked. "It doesn't work that way. Magic doesn't work that way. You're born with your element. Had you not been born to all four, then you wouldn't have been able to trigger them, as you say. These are your gifts, Iris, and Bogmall has no claim to them. Her behavior is her fault and shall be her undoing. You're not the bad guy in this scenario."

I flattened my stare at the old man. "You sound an awful lot like my sister Dahlia."

A smirk tugged at his lips. "She's the psychologist, right?"

I gave a slight nod. "But she's also the purveyor of hard truths, and she can slap a pity party right out of you by giving you a heavy dose of reality." I reached out and looped my index finger around Thomas' pinky. "Thank you for my heavy dose of hard truths and reality. It was just the thing I needed."

His smile was gentle. "Any time."

"Do you know where they put Marigold? I have to see for myself that she's all right."

Thomas pointed to a curtained-off area in the back right corner. "Over there."

"Was she still badly injured?"

"Uh, no," Thomas said. "She and Zev—"

"Thank you!" I let him go and rushed off to see her. Keir was sitting on the cot with Luanne, and they were both smiling. It warmed my heart to see their reunion. It was such a relief that Lu's injuries weren't as debilitating as Simon's.

When I got to the curtain, I heard a moan that

sounded like someone was in pain, and the warmth I'd felt seconds earlier turned to ice in my veins.

I yanked the curtain back, horrified by the sight that greeted me. Marigold was on the same cot as Zev, and they were both naked from the waist up. Whatever was happening under the blankets, I didn't want to know. I yanked the curtain closed behind me so no one else would see my sister getting jiggy with the djinn. "Marigold," I hissed.

She let out a squeak of surprise, then grabbed the blanket and pulled it up to cover her breasts as she rolled off Zev and onto the floor. I was greeted with an extremely athletic body, sporting an eager and ready stiffy. I clamped my eyes shut. "Nope." I shook my head. "What the hell is going on in here?"

"Get out, Iris," Marigold fumed. "And close the curtain behind you."

I kept my eyes closed. "This is dangerous. You both know it. Zev, you can't be with Marigold. You're an ifrit. If you bake my sister from the inside out, I'm going to kill you."

"*Sahira*," Zev said, his voice soft and seductive. "Macha took my flame. Your sister is perfectly safe and capable of making her own decisions."

"And what happens when your flame returns?" I asked.

"Then I'll deal with it," Marigold replied. "I'm not a child. I'm older than you, and I can make my own decisions."

She sounded closer, so I peeked in her direction. Marigold was a few feet from me with the sheet wrapped around her like a sarong. But something about the way she looked was all wrong.

"Did you get...taller?" I mean, my sister was always tall, but it looked as if she'd grown by more than five inches. How was this... Oh, goddess. Macha. Shit.

"We'll speak about it later," Marigold said. "But Zev, who knows a bit of history, said Queen Olwen was half-giant."

"Olwen?" Then I remembered. Macha had been going on about Olwen when she was talking to Marigold. And she said she couldn't fix her, but she could transform her. "She made you a giant?"

"Half," Marigold said.

"More like a quarter," Zev said. "But she's alive. That's what matters, no?"

I blew out a noisy breath. Zev was right, but he wasn't getting off the hook that easily. "I knew I couldn't trust you to do the right thing. Not where it's important. You deserted Keir and me out in the woods, and now, you're playing with my sister's heart. I swear to god if I could—"

"Stop it," Marigold snapped. "He didn't desert you."

I turned my glare onto my sister. "You weren't there. You don't know. Linda was in serious trouble, and Zev just disappeared."

"He didn't just disappear. Freya summoned him." Marigold's voice calmed as she said, "I was there. Zev gave Freya a token for a one-time summoning if she ever truly needed him, and she used it. He had no say in the matter." She narrowed her gaze on me. "He berated her and championed getting back to you." Her eyes sparkled with tears.

"So don't you dare wish anything bad for Zev. He has your back, even if you don't have his."

My mouth gaped open. Oh, my goddess, my sister loved him. She hardcore, forever loved him. This was so bad. But not because Zev was bad.

I turned my attention to the ifrit, who thankfully had thrown a pillow over his erection. He nodded his affirmation. "I did not desert you, *sahira*. But you're not the only one with power over where I go."

That last part was like a gut punch. "I'm sorry," I said. And it felt like I was spending a lot of time apologizing. "I'm so sorry."

I stepped back through the curtain and made sure it was closed before I walked over to Keir. He gave me a knowing look.

"You heard all that?" I asked.

"Puca hearing." He took my hand, and I sat on the edge of the cot with him and Lu. "You okay?"

"Better now. I may need some eyeball bleach later, but Marigold is good. A little taller, but good."

Luanne squinted at me. "I feel like there are whole paragraphs of information I'm missing."

I grinned and shook my head. "If..." I shook my head again. "When I survive the tests tomorrow, and we go home to Southill Village, I will give you a detailed blow-by-blow, and I'll take full creative license in spicing it up."

She cackled at my response. "I'll take you up on that."

Harry and Hellie escorted all six archdruids into the ballroom to meet with the wounded. Freya's gaze immediately settled on Keir, Luanne, and me. She walked over. "I'm so happy to see you recovering, Luanne."

Lu shrugged and said, "Thanks."

I forced my anger at her for summoning Zev as far down as I could. She hadn't known how much we'd needed him when she'd snatched him away, and I was still feeling emotionally raw from my sister calling me out on my bullshit. Now was not the time for a confrontation.

The other archdruids came our way, and the wiggle of the hag stone started the charm bracelet vibrating as it warmed my skin. I grabbed the stone to keep it from making noise. One of them was using spirit magic. Maybe possessed by the spirit of my enemy, and I couldn't let on that I knew. "Uhm, hey," I said to the grove leaders. "Making the rounds, huh?"

Yasmine Leafborn fluffed her curly hair and said, "Thanks to you, sweetheart, it's not a whole lot worse. We got lucky."

None of this had felt lucky to me. "You're welcome." My voice raised at the end like a question. I was terrible at playing it cool. "I think it's time I got upstairs to shower. I can still feel the snotgurgle on my skin."

Mathias made a face. "Get some rest, Iris Everlee. You're going to need it."

Derrick shook his head. "Be nice, Mattie. The girl just saved all of our asses."

I gave a quick smile of thanks to the Green Grove leader, then turned to Keir. "You coming?"

He stood up with me, and with a wink, he said, "Not yet."

I snorted a laugh as some of the tension eased from my shoulders.

As we left the ballroom, I didn't hazard to look back. When we were out of earshot, I turned and kissed Keir.

"What was that for?" he asked. "Not that I'm complaining."

"For being you." I booped his nose, wondering where Bob was. The imp usually showed up when I was under great emotional stress. "One of the archdruids is practicing or has been taken over by spirit magic."

"Are you sure?" Keir asked.

I rattled my bracelet at him. "Unless this thing lies."

"Well, shit."

My sentiments exactly.

# CHAPTER 20

THE DAY OF RECKONING HAD FINALLY ARRIVED. AFTER two hot showers and no sign of Linda the night before, the exhaustion and horror of the entire day had weighed heavily on me. After I'd managed to pull myself together, Keir tucked me into bed and held me until I fell asleep. God, I loved that man. He had been just the medicine I'd needed.

Of course, most medicines are only good for a few hours, and this was no exception. The rest of the night had been fitful sleep with dreams of foul creatures, blonde sorcerers, maimed gnomes, dead sisters, and terrifying gods. In other words, I was exhausted and finding it hard to think. It didn't matter to the powers-that-be because they were enthusiastic for me to start the test. On top of that, any interference from anyone, *Keir-cough-cough-Keir*, but also, they meant anyone, would not be tolerated. If Lu, Marigold, Zev, Carver, Thomas, Linda, or anyone who cared, stepped in to help me, the trials would be over, and my magic bound. Which is why I'd made Zev promise to keep Marigold at the house and away from the middle of the hedge maze. My sister wouldn't be able to stop herself from interfering. She had poor impulse control when it came to wanting to save my ass.

Late in the afternoon, I stood a few feet outside the circular henge at the center of the hedge maze, awaiting the first test of the *malificionito*. Woo-freaking-hoo.

I was placed in front of an orange, kind of sparkly, large phallus-looking stone that had been set up for my tera-craft test. The archdruids had made a sweeping decision that the ritual trials would begin at four, starting with terra-craft and ending in nero. Fine by me, I thought. The sooner I got this over with, the sooner I could go home to my house, my kid, and my bed.

I was glad I was starting with earth. It had been my first element and the one I was most confident with. I gave myself a minute to reflect on how stupid all these archdruids and their covens were and that if I never saw them again after this, it would be too soon, before placing my palm against the smooth surface.

The stone was extremely dense and cold to touch. "What kind of rock is this?" I asked.

"Feldspar. Sunstone variety. Mid-range on the hardness scale, but still a tough nut to crack," said the plump woman who'd invoked earth during the battle the night before. "Especially while the sun is still up."

Now I understood why the testing was starting right before sunset. They had wanted to make terra-craft as hard as possible on me. Whatever. I had this, I told myself. I freaking had this. I felt around the surface of the sunstone for some kind of opening or weakness. There were none. With false bravado, I said, "I've cracked tougher nuts."

The woman grinned, revealing the deep dimples on either side of her rosy cheeks. "Unfortunately, nut cracking won't be in the job description."

Dang it, I didn't want to like her. She was part of the machine that was making me do this stupid *malificionito*. But I couldn't help myself, she was funny.

She thrust her hand at me. My bracelet wasn't buzzing, so I accepted her offer of a handshake. "I'm Darla Edwards," she said. "Such a pleasure to meet you." She smiled at me. "I'm rooting for you."

Derrick came forward then. "You will have until sunset to complete the first trial."

"What do you want me to do?" Blowing shit up was my specialty, so I hoped they were looking for fireworks.

They were not.

"Inside the stone is a rare uncut red diamond that is four carats in size. You must remove it from the sunstone."

"Okay, cool." I gulped down the hot lump in my throat. "That shouldn't be too hard, eh?"

"And," Derrick continued, "You must do it without damaging the sunstone or utilizing any of your other abilities."

My eyes widened. "Uhm...okay." Man, these people really wanted to see me fail. I glanced at Keir. His face was fixed with hard lines, including this thin frown. He was pissed. I could tell he was ready to go full-on homicidal rabbit on them at any moment. He was itching for an excuse.

I'd been lucky enough to have a task-master gnome named Linda as my teacher. She'd made me learn how to tune my body's matter to the frequency of a solid rock and move through it. The rocks in question, though, were made of much more porous material than the stone standing before me. And, to date, I'd only been able to get a few fingers through without help from Linda.

Thinking of the gnome made my heart sink. I'd never wanted to be beaned in the head with a rock, like ever. But if it meant having Linda back whole again, I would gladly suffer a hundred concussions. I swallowed my fear. If Linda was here, she would say, "Stupid, *Kleinkind*. Just get the diamond. Don't think. Do."

"All right, Linda," I muttered. "This one's for you." I measured the girth of the stone. I would need to go into the rock up to my elbow to reach the center. Yikes. The stone was opaque, so I wasn't sure how I was going to find it. It dawned on me that if feldspar was mid-range hardness and diamonds were the hardest stones, then all I really needed to do was match the sunstone's frequency and ignore the diamond until I was inside. "In and out."

I had dressed in comfy workout clothes, including leggings, an oversized tank, and a light jacket. I pushed up the sleeves of the jacket and then set my palm against the stone again. This process wasn't about incantations or using herbs and minerals for a potion. This was physiology 101, and I was a C student. Still, average was better than failing.

I slapped the feldspar, then flattened my palm against the stone to measure the vibrations against my skin. It was definitely different than the agate I practiced with back home.

"What is she doing?" I heard Derrick ask.

"I'm not sure," Darla answered. "It looks like she's spanking the rock. It must've been a very naughty boy."

If I hadn't been so incredibly frustrated, I might've laughed. I shushed them. "I need silence, please. At least give me that courtesy."

The druids and witches got quieter, but I could still hear a few murmurs in the crowd. I slapped the stone again. This time, I could feel the reverberations, almost like echoes, travel into my fingers and my palm. My hand slipped into the rock.

There were several surprised gasps, and the murmuring grew louder as I matched the frequency to my wrist. *Please let this work*, I silently chanted.

When my wrist slid inside, there were a few appreciative claps. Great, I had some fans. The only consolation was knowing that a lot of people, especially the ones at Iron Grove, wanted me to succeed.

The forearm was more fat and muscle than bone, so it took me a moment to modulate my wavelength to match the sunstone, but finally, I was elbow-deep in the big orange penis.

I flashed to Zev from the night before as I felt around inside for the diamond. I was going to need brain-draino to get that monster out of my head, and I wasn't talking about the ifrit. Well, not his entire self.

When I finally came up against the diamond, my hand kept slipping around it. Crap. I hadn't really thought this through. How was I going to move the diamond through the stone? I had matched the feldspar frequency, but for the diamond, it was just as hard as it had been when it had been formed in the mineral.

"Everything all right?" Darla asked sweetly.

Liking her was no longer a problem. "It's all good," I said.

Damn it, the sun was starting to set, and I was losing daylight fast.

The gathered crowd had grown eerily quiet as they waited for me to shit or get off the pot.

Again, I asked myself, WWLD? What would Linda do? There was only one thing I could think of trying, and that was forcing the diamond to the same frequency as the sunstone. But would that ruin the diamond? Would they consider that a failure? Even if I could manage, how would I get it out? My hand would pass right through the diamond then. I wouldn't be able to hold it. Unless I *could* hold it. The idea took shape in my mind. What if I could wrap my fingers around the diamond close enough that it acted as a vehicle.

I closed my fist around it and concentrated on moving it. It budged an inch, and I let out a triumph, "Yes!"

"Did she get it out?" someone asked.

"I don't think so," another replied.

The murmuring grew loud once more, but I didn't care. The freaking diamond was moving. It was slow going, but it was going. The fact that I was racing a sun that wouldn't slow down made me sweat, though. Just a little bit more, I thought. My wrist was free. Next, the base of my hand, and finally, my whole fist, was out.

"Well?" Darla asked with eager anticipation. "Let's see it?"

I turned my hand over and opened my fingers. In the cup of my palm was a perfectly clean, uncut four-carat red diamond. "Do I get to keep it?"

Darla giggled. "You'll have to fight Derrick for it."

I raised a brow at the archdruid.

He shook his head and smirked. "If you survive all four tests, the diamond is yours."

There was a rousing cheer of excitement from the gathered throng.

Derrick held up his hands to silence them. "The Green Grove is satisfied that Iris Everlee has mastered terra-craft. She showed a skill I have never seen matched." He sounded genuinely happy at my success.

One down, three to go.

As I waited for the ignis-craft trial to begin, the two witches I'd seen on the battlefield the night before, one from Bezoar, the other from Shining River, came to stand by me. Mathias's man was a lanky blond named Terry Nettles. The dude had greasy hair, much like his archdruid. I wondered if they shared grooming products. The other was a tall, thin brunette that I had mistaken for a female during the battle because of their feminine features and their long dark hair. Their name was Obi Darkflame, a two-spirit, meaning neither male nor female, witch.

"So, Obi," I asked the witch as I eyeballed what

looked like a pile of logs up against a wooden pole. "Are you planning to burn me to see if I survive?"

They gave me a look that told me I was correct.

"Fantastic." I turned to Terry. "I suppose you'll be first in line to throw the match."

"I'm more a gasoline and a flamethrower kind of guy," Terry answered.

"A wise guy, huh?"

He chuckled, but not in a friendly way.

Yikes. Once again, I glanced over at Keir. There was a sneer on his face, and if stares could kill, Terry would be dead.

Mathias and Yasmine held up their hands to quiet the crowd, much the same as Derrick had.

Mathias went first. "Iris Everlee must escape the flame unharmed."

Okay, got it. Easy-peasy, lemon squeezy. I'd escaped a volcano. I really wasn't too worried about a bonfire harming me.

Terry and Obi walked me to the top of the log pile and tied me to the pole. Yep, it was a good old-fashioned witch-burning. This was seriously revolting and in seriously poor taste.

Yasmine Leafborne spoke next. "You must show your mastery of fire," she said to me, "by using only ignis-craft to manage flame and heat to protect a life."

"Protect a life?" I swore to all that was profane that I would wreck their world if they put someone's life in danger merely to get me to quit the game.

Obi placed a metal stand on the pile, then Terry

carried a round fishbowl with a goldfish the size of a golf ball swimming around inside it. He set it on the stand.

"You have got to be freaking kidding me," I protested.

Then Obi poured the gasoline, and Terry lit the fire. The greasy blond tipped his head to me. "Better hurry." He tugged at the collar of his shirt. "It's starting to get hot."

A growl of frustration tore from my lips. Terry was a turd, and I hated his guts. Unfortunately, he didn't make my charm bracelet dance, or I would have happily exploded his head from his body. He'd find out exactly how hot it could get.

My hands were tied behind my back, making it impossible to use my hands to control the flames. The fire was starting to creep higher. As it neared the fishbowl, I struggled harder against the ropes. "Hang on, Goldie. I'm coming for you."

The fish swam back and forth, frantically searching for a way out. "You people are sick," I shouted.

"We can halt the trial," Mathias said. "Just say the word."

"Kiss my ass!"

The expression on his face told me those were not the words he had been hoping would come out of my mouth.

I hit the bindings on my hands and legs with fire that poured off my fingertips. The ropes would not burn through. What in the world was happening? Had they tied me up with some flameproof twine? The bonfire began to dance around the fishbowl, licking at its sides. How much time did the goldfish have? I wished I could ask someone how long it takes to boil water, but I worried the archdruids would consider that "help."

I was great at ignis-craft, and I was failing. I was failing myself, Keir, my family, and I was failing Goldie the Goldfish.

The fish's movements became sluggish. The water was heating up, and if I didn't figure this out quick, Goldie would not be long for this world.

I had killed a world destroyer. Gods sure did love their titles, and Volres, the fire god, was no exception. But he'd sorely underestimated my will to live and my will to save a life. My grimoire had told me to embrace the fire, and I embraced it hard. I sucked the core from Volres, and for a moment, I had been as a god. A minor one, of course, but the power had been frightening and wonderful for about two seconds. Then it had almost turned me into something I wouldn't survive, so I'd purged myself of him.

I didn't need my hands, I finally realized. I never did. "Fire," I said. And when it ignored me, I screamed, "Fire!" The blaze flared up in response. I gave the dancing flames a dark command, "Mine," I told it. "Every bit is mine." I opened my mouth and inhaled, calling the fire to me. Suddenly, I was the flame, and the bonfire was the moth as it left the logs in a steady stream to pour down my throat. The heat didn't burn. It energized me, and my arms blackened as if remembering when I was a god. My veins turned bright red, glowing beneath my charred skin. Once again, the power of the earth's magma core flowed through my blood. I yanked both of my hands free of the binding and stepped out of the ropes around my legs as they fell apart in my wake.

"I have passed your test," I intoned in a voice that was ominously not my own. I staggered off the smoldering wood pile and then purged the flames into a nearby trash-can. It lit up like a hobo winter event. After, I walked over to Goldie and picked up the bowl. The fish, still fearing for its life—and who could blame it—swam from one side to the other, still looking for an exit. "Your safe now," I told it. "No one will harm you."

Terry the Terrible walked over and tried to take the fish from me.

I hugged the bowl to my body. "No!" I said sternly. "Just no."

He backed away from me, no longer smug after witnessing my fire-eating skills.

I gave him an *I dare you* glare, then added, "Goldie has a new home now." I walked her or him because I had no idea how to sex a goldfish, over to Keir and handed the bowl off. "Kill anyone who tries to take the fish."

Keir's eyes turned puca-black, and he nodded. "Done."

I whipped around to face Mathias and Yasmine. "The fish is mine. Spoils of my labor."

"Of course," Yasmine said. And before Mathias could open his mealy mouth, she added, "Iris Everlee has satis-fied Shining River and Bazoar Grove. She has control and mastery of fire."

"Agreed," Mathias said blandly.

"Good," I told them. "Two down, two to go."

# CHAPTER 21

I GAVE THOMAS THE STINK-EYE AS I STARED UPWARD IN dismay. "What's with the giant, fifty-foot tall metal pole with the platform for?" The pole had rungs sticking out on either side, going all the way to the tippy top.

"I'm not allowed to say," he offered quickly. "That would be against the rules."

The woman, an aero-craft witch, named Vicky, whom I'd seen next to Jerriah Dale the night before, gave me a look and said, "Molly, you in danger, girl."

I had to fight an absurd giggle at the Whoopie Goldberg *Ghost* reference.

"What am I supposed to do?"

"Climb," she said.

I frowned. "How far?"

She pointed to the sky. "All the way up."

"This is nuts."

"You're telling me," she said. "I'm glad I didn't have to do all this bullshit when I sparked. This is barbaric."

"About as barbaric as agreeing to bind my powers if I

186

don't pass the groves' standards, and it doesn't kill me in the process."

Vicky had the good sense to blush. Thomas gave me a pat on the back. "I have faith in you, Iris."

"That makes one of us."

"Go ahead and climb," he said. "The test will begin when you get to the top."

"Perfect." I grabbed the first metal wrung. "This is stupidly dangerous."

The old air practitioner didn't quarrel. "Understood and agreed."

In my heart, I knew this wasn't Thomas' fault. He was a bystander in the process. It hadn't been his decision or choice for me to be tested. It hurt that he was participating. Like me, he probably didn't have a choice either. Still, it seems like he could've given me some hints as to what I would need to know when it came to this climbing the pole test.

Maybe that was it. I probably had to get to the top and stand there using air magic to keep me upright. I could do that. Okay, I coached myself. Get your ass up there and get it over with.

Keir had handed the goldfish off to his sister Lu. I think he wanted both arms open in case I couldn't balance. It wasn't bad thinking. I was a klutz by nature. If I didn't pass this test, it wouldn't be about how much control I had over my magic. It would be because I could trip over absolutely nothing.

"I'll be careful," I assured him. I knew he was dialed into my voice. "Trust me to handle this."

I met his gaze, and he gave me a slow nod that he got

the message loud and clear.

The farther up the pole I got, the more the damn thing swayed. The motion made me feel icky in the tummy. *Lord*, the last thing I needed was to vomit from fifty feet up over a crowd of onlookers. Of course, there were many betting on whether I lived or died or had my magic stripped, so maybe they deserved a little spew.

*Keep climbing,* I told myself. *You are halfway home free. Just get through these last two tests.* Yeah, only two. The two I was least confident with.

At one point, my foot slipped off a rung, and I heard a collective "whoa," from below. I gripped tightly with my hands and got my footing solid, then yelled, "I'm okay!" But who was I kidding? I was far from okay. Fifty feet doesn't seem like much when you're talking high rises, but as the pole swayed and the druids and witches got smaller, I could swear I'd never been so high in my life.

Finally, I made it to the top. The platform was tricky to maneuver onto, and there was a two-inch thick antenna jutting up from the center that I could hold onto to pull myself up. It was only a foot wide, and with the stabilizing pole in the middle, there was not much room for sitting. Would they want me to stand? Probably, the bastards. The thought made me woozy.

The Harvest moon was a rusty red, and its glow had turned the white henge stones pink. It was a beautiful and petrifying view. It was dark enough outside the stones that it was hard to see Keir. "Now what?" I yelled down, eager to get this over with.

Thomas, who was now inside the henge near the altar, gave me a "stay there" hand signal. Freya stood below me now, along with Jerriah Dale. Jerriah held up his hands and said, "Ms. Everlee must exert precise control over her aero-craft in this test. It is designed to simulate high stress, something that Ms. Everlee has demonstrated often leads her to lose control, causing chaos, damage, and danger to innocent bystanders."

Sure, drain one little stock pond, and, all of a sudden, all the fish in it are innocent bystanders.

Not going to lie. I did feel guilty about the bass. And, to be honest, the fish hadn't been the only beings I'd put in direct danger over the past few months because of my unpredictability.

"Fair point," I shouted down to him.

In my defense, though, I usually started out a little chaotic but had always managed to rein my ability in with time. I'd grown much more confident in my air magic in just a few short weeks. Did I trust it to keep me standing on this moving pole? Uhm, sure.

Freya stepped up to deliver part two of my trial.

"Jump!" she yelled up to me.

Even from this high up, I heard gasps coming from the audience.

I refused to believe my ears, so I asked, "Say again?"

"Jump," Freya repeated. "If you can stop yourself before you hit the ground, you pass the test."

"You've got to be fuckin' kidding me," I muttered. About twenty feet away, I saw Fair Konig zipping back and forth nervously as he watched me contemplate my death. The pixie king was smart enough to stay silent and not help, but knowing he was there did bring me some comfort.

I looked down and immediately regretted it. "It's not the fall that gets you. It's the landing."

"You have thirty seconds," Jerriah added. "Jump or climb down. Either way, this trial is about to end."

Thirty seconds? I couldn't count and formulate a plan of action. How in the world was I to know when thirty seconds was up.

"Twenty-five, twenty-four, twenty-three," the crowd sang out.

If possible, their counting down to my doom made it even harder to think. I wasn't sure what I could do with air that would cushion a blow from this high up. Chances were super good I would break my back on one of the henge stones before I even hit the ground. I pushed the unpleasant thought aside.

"Fifteen, fourteen, thirteen," the onlookers continued. A few of them had started chanting, "Jump, jump, jump." Those sons—and daughters—of bitches.

Once again, I had a big decision to make. With earth and fire, it had been an easy choice. I knew I could handle those elements. Air was giving me gas.

Oh. Gas. Helium rises. If only there was a clown nearby with a hundred floating balloons.

"Nine, eight, seven...."

Fair Konig was darting back and forth, his worry and fear apparent. He was my air guardian, and we'd had little time to practice the way Linda and I had. And what of Linda? I owed her so much. If I died, I wouldn't get to say goodbye. On the other hand, if they nullified my magic, she could never say goodbye back. And what of Bob? My floofy imp would probably disappear back to wherever imps go when they are no longer needed.

"Five, four...."

"Shut up!" I screamed at the morbid horde.

"Two," they called out, and without another thought, I leaped off the platform and into the air...

...and I fell to my death.

Until I didn't. I called the air below, above and around me to heed my call, and a rush of wind below me slowed my dissent. The way Fair Konig used his rapidly beating wings to hover like a helicopter gave me the next part of my plan, and I gathered blades of air above my hands and tethered them to my fingers as the ground rose up below me quicker than I could manage.

But the blades began to spin, and I felt the first real tug of resistance, and when I was several feet from breaking both my legs, I flung the blades below my feet, and the move launched me several yards upward so that when I finally landed, I was able to roll away without more than a few scratches. Nothing I couldn't heal from.

And, I might add, without destroying any buildings, mountains, or people in the process.

I got up and dusted my leggings off. "What now, bitches?"

Freya raised her brow at me, and I shrugged. If people didn't want to be called bitches, then they shouldn't act like bitches.

"The Iron Grove is satisfied that Iris Everlee does have proper control of aero-craft. She has passed the third trial.

I turned my gaze to Jerriah Dale, daring him to say

differently. The archdruid merely nodded. "Mountain Ash Grove concurs."

Hah. Three down, one to go.

IT WAS eleven o'clock before they finished setting up the water torture chamber for the fourth and final trial. Fun. Fun. Earlier I'd been grateful it was the last test, but now I wished it had been the first. Like removing a bandaid, it would have been better to rip it off and get the pain over quick. As it was, if I couldn't manage to get my nero-craft under control, I was going to end my run as a tru-crafter by drowning. This was just another sick play off the old-school witch trials of dunking witches. If you weren't a witch, you drowned. If you were a witch and survived, they burned you at the stake. A bit like they'd tried to do to Goldie and me earlier. I was beginning to hate the mega-mansion and all its luxury. All I wanted was to be home in my own bed, snuggled with Keir and Bob. Linda would be out in the garden doing garden gnome stuff. My kid living his best senior year life. My sister.... Okay, my sister was a giantess now. That was going to be hard to explain to Dad. Even Dahlia, Rowan, and Rose were going to have some trouble processing the news. Still, she was alive, and we would all be together.

*Pie in the sky thinking*, I admonished myself. *Keep your thoughts in the present if you want to survive.*

But how? I'd tried to call a simple brook to do my bidding the night before, and instead, I'd transported an entire body of water over a mile to my location. Zero control. Zero! Well, okay. Not zero. The pond landed where it needed to land. Linda was saved at the expense of some fish. Again, guilt. But I would take out a hundred ponds if it meant saving my girl.

*Oh, Linda, where are you?* I hoped on hope that she'd managed to make it back home to her Donzy. Imagining her with her husband and her people was the only thing that kept me from crying.

Carver stood near Keir now. He gave me a wave. I wondered if he was half-baked, and if he was, I wondered if it was possible he'd brought an extra gummy with him. I'd never been one to really do a lot of drugs, but if ever an occasion called for it, it was now.

Telva Mack, Luna Grove's archdruid, was near the water tomb with her coven witch Corina, their heads bent in quiet conversation. I turned to Keir. He shook his head, indicating he couldn't hear anything they were saying. I had been near every archdruid and their tru-craft witch during the trials, and none of them had set off my spirit alarm. Which meant, Telva and Corina were the final pieces. One of them was using anima-craft or was being used by it. It was bad enough the chamber might kill me because my water magic sucked, but the idea that I would have to fight off a spirit attack as well meant my chances of surviving this one were not good.

I rubbed the hag stone on my bracelet as I picked my chin up and brought my shoulders back. No way was I going to let them know I was scared for my life. Of course, only an idiot would've felt safe. I was no idiot... said the woman walking to her watery grave.

"Iris Everlee will enter the water chamber," Telva said

to the crowd. "She will use only nero-craft to escape. If she fails to exit the chamber in ten minutes, she forfeits the trial."

The joke was on her. I could barely hold my breath for two minutes. If I didn't exit the chamber in ten minutes, chances were good I was dead.

Corina gestured to the ladder on the side of the glass structure. It was already full to the top with clear water and no breathing room to spare. Lovely. At least, unlike Houdini, they weren't planning on putting me inside the tank upside down.

"Climb in," the tiny blonde witch said.

I purposefully brushed past her to see if my bracelet would go off, but it stayed inactive. Corina wasn't the spirit user. Well, poop. I sidestepped around her so that I could pass near Telva Mack. Again, nothing happened.

I was sure it was one of the archdruids. They'd been near both times that the bracelet had signaled anima-craft being used. This was both good and terrible. Good, because it meant Bogmall wasn't in charge of the water torture. That could've been really bad. And terrible because the hexen-piece-of-shit was still out there, some-where in this crowd, taking immense pleasure at my expense.

"I just climb on in?" I asked, stalling for a little time. I had no basis of knowledge or past experience to get me through this one. I was completely on my own.

Keir's eyes were black with worry, and even Carver, who was normally zen, was fidgety. Crap on toast. I was really screwed.

I'd come too far to stop now.

I climbed up the ladder and was pleasantly surprised to find that the water in the chamber was warm and not freezing. At least my death would be comfortable. Hah.

Corina gestured to Hellie and Harry to come and help her close the lid. When the twins reached up, my bracelet was above the water line as I grasped the edge. It began to vibrate and warm against my skin. My eyes widened as the lid closed on my head. I dropped my hand down, and the vibration stopped. I was so rattled I didn't take a good breath, and I ended up swallowing salt water.

Saltwater?

Hellie smiled at me and then tapped the glass. I heard her voice in my head. *Salt nullifies charms, Iris. No one will know, and you won't be around to tell them. Enjoy your death. I know I will.*

# CHAPTER 22

WATCHING HELLIE, AKA BOGMALL, WALK AWAY WITH that smug expression made me want to scream. Unfortunately, I barely had any air in my lungs, and now that I was underwater, I had more immediate problems than a power-hungry sorcerer.

The saltwater made me buoyant, so I naturally floated at the top. My ass, which had a little more fat in it than my chest, was pressed against the ceiling of the vault. It would've been embarrassing. Even so, I had to figure out a way to warn Keir that Bogmall was wearing Hellie's skin. There had been subtle hints but nothing overt. Bogmall had played the role well, and why wouldn't she? She'd been Hellie, Harry, and Luanne's chief for many years. She knew the warrior druids well enough to pass.

I banged on the glass and tried to point, but my top, a loose-flowing yoga-style tank, slid up my torso and over my head. It trapped me in a weblike snare, and panic started to set in.

"Calm," I remembered Keir telling me when we

were sparring. "Adrenaline will get you killed," he said. "You have to find a way to keep your fight or flight reflexes in check." This wasn't the same situation, but my fear had punched my heart rate into overdrive, passing through my lungs quickly and depleting me of air.

Speaking of air, I struggled to fight the impulse to employ aero, terra, and ignis craft to facilitate my escape. I stripped my shirt over my head and pushed it away from me just in time to see Hellie walking to the exit into the hedge maze. She turned around and smiled at me. My body tingled, and I felt light-headed as her magic permeated my skin.

*Poor, poor, Iris,* she cooed in my brain. *Always one step behind me. Just like the day we were born.*

The day we were born? I didn't understand.

*Of course, you don't. Always the favorite. Always the one that had to be saved no matter the cost.*

Her arrogant expression made my throat clench.

*But not anymore. I have my own magic now, and I will have what rightfully should've been mine in the first place.* Her gaze pivoted to Keir. *And the minute you take your last breath, that's when I will take you, and I will rot your relationships with everyone and everything that you love.*

*You're a fool,* I thought. I directed my thoughts to Bogmall. I wasn't sure if she could hear me the way I heard her, but I wanted to be super clear with the delusional bitch. *Have you learned nothing? I don't die. I survive. And threatening my family has ensured your destruction.*

I sipped the water into my mouth. The liquid curled around my tongue, tasting like salty tears. I could control my tears. I could control water. I was a nero-craft witch, and this was just another day for me.

I used the water around me to push me until I was upright in a standing position. I pressed my fingertips against the glass and called upon the salty liquid to spin like a drill against the thick set pane.

I saw the crowd stepping back and away. I looked at Keir, and his fingers had turned into black diamond claws, ready to cut me out of the tank if necessary. I gave him a headshake, but he didn't put the claws away. Good. He would need them in about a minute when I got out of here and went after Bogmall. I'd hold her down while he sliced and diced.

Water jets were used to cut thick glass in a way that left smooth edges, and I called to the water in my body to match the water in the tank, and I dropped to my knees on the bottom of the tank. I used my fingertips to cut a large laser-precise circle near waist level.

That wiped the smug look right off the bitch. *I'm coming for you,* I told her. *There isn't a place on earth you can hide.*

Water shot out of the chamber from the cut I'd created, and when I got to the bottom edge, the circle snapped, and the glass shot five feet as the water carried me out onto the grass.

It took a second for my lungs to adjust to air, but once I could speak, I pointed to Hellie. "Stop her!"

"Who?" Keir asked.

"Hellie," I said. "Hellie is Bogmall."

*Well-played, sister*, she said in my head, u*ntil the next time*. At her parting words, Hellie passed out.

AFTER THE WATER TRIAL, Telva Mack declared that Luna Grove considered me safe to practice nero-craft. I'd declared that I didn't give a shit what she or any of the other archdruids and their respective groves thought about me and my ability to practice magic. As far as I was concerned, they could go screw themselves. If I ever saw any of them again, it would be too soon, including Freya. They'd put me through the wringer, and I wasn't about to forgive or forget.

When Hellie had passed out, Bogmall had escaped. The druid warrior, unlike Yolanda, remembered very little of her time being possessed. She'd fought against Bogmall's control until the ex-druid turned sorcerer had shut down all of the woman's awareness. Harry confessed that he'd thought his sister was acting strange. But Hellie had been on a mission for six months, and he'd written her odd behavior off as related to a bad op. She hadn't wanted to talk about it. He hadn't pressed the issue. Harry's guilt was exponential.

I had my own issues to contend with. Bogmall had called me sister. She'd alluded to the fact that she was born right before me, but on the same day. We looked nothing alike, so I found it hard to believe she wasn't telling more lies. Still, there was something about what she said that rang true.

If the woman was trying to unnerve me, she was succeeding. One thing I knew for certain, I could no longer wait for the hexen-bitch to come after me. It was time to take the offensive. Taking her down was the only way I could keep the people I loved safe. Luckily, the Green Grove archdruid had kept his word. I'd survived the trials, and the red diamond worth more money than I could make in a lifetime was mine. Once I sold it, I'd have enough money to quit my job for a little while and focus on finding Bogmall. On top of that, Michael was going to be able to go to any college he wanted. Bonus.

"You about ready?" Keir asked as he came back to our room.

I was almost finished packing my bags. Bob had shown up right after my shower, and he'd been purring loud and steady like a car with a hole in the muffler. Still, I found it comforting.

I gave my chonky monster a scritch between the ears. "Thanks, Bob." He gave me a slow blink of welcome.

"I got fish food for Goldie," Keir said. "You sure you want to take her home. You know they don't live long."

"I walked through fire for her, so as long as she's alive, she's living with me," I told him. "Is Marigold ready to go? I don't want her driving home alone."

"Zev, Luanne, and Fair Konig are doing the trip with her." He wrapped his arms around me from behind and kissed the tip of my ear. "Zev is going to stay in Southill Village until we figure out how to force Bogmall out into the open."

I nodded. "Good." The ifrit still didn't have his fire, but all the rest of his djinn powers were present and accounted for. "We'll need him."

"Linda?" he asked.

I shook my head and fought back the tears. "Still nothing. I called Michael. He said she's not in the garden.

I hope she's with her family, but I don't know how to find out. It's not like she's got a cellphone."

"She'll be okay," he assured me as he held me tighter. "We'll find her. We will."

"Promise?" I asked.

"You have my word," he swore.

And I had him. The blonde bitch acted as if he should've been hers. "Did you ever go out with Bogmall?"

I felt his chin jerk in a surprised tuck. "Uhm, no. Not at all."

"Okay." I reached back and patted his cheek. "Just asking. She seems to have a thing for you."

"Weird. I never noticed."

Men could be oblivious. "Do you really think she's my sister? You saw my birth. Did you see hers?"

He shook his head. "Only you. I only ever saw you."

The fact that we might be related made me feel ill. "I have all the sisters I want. Blood or no blood, Bogmall is no sister of mine."

I picked my grimoire up off the bed and remembered what it had said:

*Blood of my blood, you must break the ties.*

*Tears of my tears, seek the truth in the lies.*

*A test of skill is a test of will. Do not fail, or it will kill.*

*The waters ahead are uncharted, and the tide won't easily stop once it has started.*

*Goddess, help you.*

Was Bogmall my twin? Was that the truth in the lies? The test of skill was pretty self-explanatory. I'd killed those tests. One thing the book definitely got right, I was moving into uncharted territory. The hunted was going to become the hunter, and I was going to make the sorcerer regret the day she darkened my door.

Until then, I was going to go home, hug my kid, and sleep for a solid eight hours. Everything else could wait until tomorrow.

A tingle rippled across my skin, reminiscent of when Bogmall had hit me with spirit magic, only this time, the tingle was warm and gentle.

Keir let me go. "Are you all right?"

Even Bob got up and moved a couple feet away.

The loose hairs around my head floated as if full of static electricity, and an apparition shot out of the grimoire cover. It was the bronze woman who had warned me to trust my head and not my emotions.

"Who are you?" I asked as her head seemed to be resting on the grimoire's cover.

She opened her mouth to speak, but nothing came out. She looked as if she were being strangled, but how? She wasn't real. "Tell me who you are?" I commanded her. "Tell me what you want?"

Her eyes widened, and in a low, choked voice, she said, "Beware the father." After, she immediately disappeared.

"What the hell was that?" Keir asked. He'd seen her too, and by his expression, he was just as freaked out as I was.

"I have no idea." I set the grimoire down as if it were a snake ready to bite me. On the cover, at the very top of the other four elemental signs, a circle formed. I turned my horrified gaze to Keir.

"Anima," he whispered. "You have the fifth element."

I choked on a maniacal laugh that was wrenched from my throat.

A fifth element. I had spirit magic. The rarest and most dangerous tru-craft magic.

"Oh, shit."

This was not going to be a fun ride, but it was one that I was going to see through no matter what. People counted on me. People I loved and couldn't live without. I would master anima the same way I mastered all the rest. Would it be messy? Sure. Sloppily done? I wouldn't expect anything else. Would I eventually kick its ass? Oh, yeah. At least, that was the story I was telling myself. Otherwise, I'd never get out of bed again.

THE END....UNTIL **the exciting conclusion to this five-part series Ghost in the Spell, coming February 2023.**

**Ghost in the Spell**

## You've Got Tail
## (Peculiar Mysteries and Romances Book 1)

**Kidnapping, murder, romance, and a town full of people hiding the truth will keep Sunny Haddock busy as she tries to unravel the strange happenings in Peculiar.**

\*\*\*\*\*

Moving from California to a small town called Peculiar in the Ozark's with my BFF Chavvah Trimmel should've been a total fun-fest. But then her older brother goes missing and our plans are put on hold.

That is until she mysteriously texts me for help before going completely radio-silent.

I'd always heard small town people are friendly and welcoming, but that isn't my experience. These locals are not only unfriendly, they're downright hostile.

Even Chavvah's hot younger brother Babel strongly suggests that I haul my butt back where I came from.

I'm undeterred.

I'm not about to go anywhere until I find out what happened to my bestie and her brother and solve the mystery this town is trying so hard to hide.

I may be psychic, but it doesn't take a fortune teller to see things are about to get real hairy in Peculiar!

### Sense and Scent Ability
### (A Nora Black Midlife Psychic Mystery Book 1)

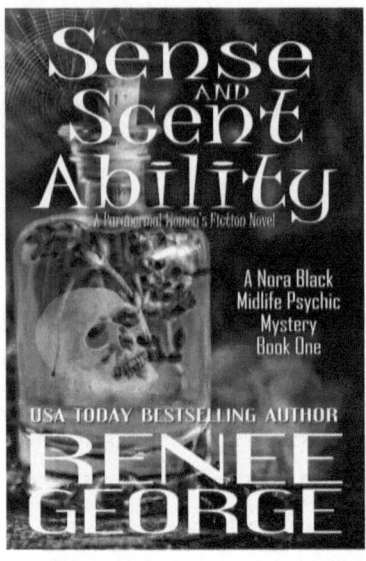

**MY NAME IS NORA BLACK, and I'm fifty-one-years young. At least that's what I tell myself, when I'm not having hot flashes, my knees don't hurt, and I can find my reading glasses.**

I'm also the proud owner of a salon called Scents & Scentsability in the small resort town of Garden Cove, where I make a cozy living selling handmade bath and beauty products. All in all, my life's is pretty good.

Except for one little glitch...

Since my recent hysterectomy, where I died on the operating table, I've been experiencing what some might call paranormal activity. No, I don't see dead people, but quite suddenly I'm triggered by scents that, in their wake, leave behind these vividly intense memories. Sometimes they're unfocused and hazy, but there's no doubt, they are very, very real.

Know what else? They're not my memories. It seems I've lost a uterus and gained a psychic gift.

When my best friend Gilly's abusive boyfriend ends up dead after a fire, and she becomes the prime suspect, I end up a babysitter to her two teenagers while she's locked up in the clink. Add to that my super sniffer's newly acquired abilities and a rash of memories connected to the real criminal, and I find myself in a race to catch a killer before my best friend is tried for murder.

# YOU'VE GOT TAIL

PECULIAR MYSTERIES & ROMANCES
BOOK 1

## Chapter One

**SOME PEOPLE JUMP** into the deep end of the pool feet first, some head first, but I've always been a traditional belly-flopper. Splashy, messy, and usually painful. Which still didn't explain why I was sitting on the floor of a closed diner, nursing my bruised butt, not to mention my pride, and staring woefully at a naked unconscious man in the middle of Peculiar, Missouri.

My parents are crazy from way back. Maybe that's where I get it from. Seriously, who names a child Ambrosia Sunshine? Two hippies, that's who. They told me when I was old enough to resent the flower child name that they'd thought it was cool at the time, but I personally believe it was the result of one too many 'shrooms. As it is, I've been forced to sit through many painful renditions of "You Are My Sunshine." If I had a dead body for every time I was teased, well, let's just say I'd get an express pass to the electric chair. Although, if I got a sympathetic judge, he'd probably consider my life-time served.

Maybe my parents' experimentation with drugs is what had made me psychic. (No, I didn't say psychotic. I said *psychic*.) On the other hand, it could also explain why I'm so bad at it.

My ability allows me glimpses, more like screenshots, of the past, present, and future. But, clearly, the visions have *not* been helpful over the years. And the side effects, sheesh. Most of the time I feel a little dizzy when they hit, but every once in a while, it's as if someone has taken a sledgehammer to the inside of my skull. Usually, I can feel one coming on; otherwise driving might be an issue. If only they made medic-alert bracelets for my type of ailment. It certainly hasn't been a gift.

That's why my friendship with Chavvah Trimmel is so important. We'd met at the community college in San Diego. She thought my name was weird and awesome all rolled up into a spring roll. After finding out her family's propensity for strange biblical names, I thought it was a bit of the pot calling the kettle rusty. Chavvah, or Chav, as she likes to be called, was my first best friend. And when she's around me, my psychic mojo kicks up twenty notches. It's as if I can tap into some kind of mystic hotline whenever she's near.

As a matter of fact, the last time I'd gotten a clear vision had been in my dining room back in California. Chav, who'd been renting my spare bedroom at the time, had just turned down the heat on the spaghetti sauce, and I was setting the table. We were having an "I finally dumped the cheating bastard" celebratory dinner. Did I mention I'm a bad psychic? So I hadn't a clue what I was walking in on when I caught my boyfriend of three years having sex with the skank waitress from the coffee shop. On my couch, no less. Jerk. I took his spare key and kicked his ass (and the couch) to the curb.

At dinner that night, when the vision hit me, I'd hit the ground, along with some clattering dishes. I saw a present moment of Chav's parents huddled together, debating whether to call her about her missing brother. Talk about being the bearer of bad news. I didn't blame her for not believing me at first, or the stunned look she gave me when she called her parents, and it turned out to be true. Her brother Judah had dropped off the map.

Chav flew back to Missouri the next day. After a year of searching for him, the local police had pretty much given up on Judah, but by that time, Chav had forgotten about the ocean and fallen in love with the little town of Peculiar. Hell, from her letters and phone calls, I'd kind of fallen in love with the place as well. She'd found a restaurant in the rural town, a real fixer-upper, for the two of us to run. A fifty-fifty partner split.

I wasn't supposed to leave California for another two weeks, and Chav had said she needed to talk to me "in person" before I made the trip, but the text I'd gotten from her had sent me packing in a hurry.

All it said was: *Sunny. I need u.*

After that, every call I'd made to Chav went straight to voice mail. Without any real plan, I jumped into my gas-guzzling Toyota 4X4, which I had purchased explicitly for the move. One thousand six hundred and sixty-two point four miles later, as I drove over a swinging bridge (the only way in and out, I soon discovered) into the quaint little town, my whole body heaved a sigh of relief. I felt strangely wonderful. It was as if someone unzipped my off-the-rack skin and fitted me with a tailored Sunny suit.

The town looked very similar to Mayberry from *The Andy Griffith Show*. Dirt streets, old fashioned shops and houses, white picket fences, and lots of Chevy and Ford pickup trucks. I was a little nervous when my GPS said, "You have arrived," right outside a two-story yellow building on the corner of Third Street and Main.

My heart pounded as I stood outside our restaurant for the first time. I'd always expected some kind of fanfare. Chav waiting to usher me into our future. She'd even named the restaurant for me. Sunny's Outlook. I'd blame allergies for my eyes watering at that moment, but I knew it was a mixture of happiness and sadness all rolled into one big bundle. This was *our* place. Mine and Chav's. And she'd done it up spectacularly.

I smiled at the brightly colored lettering. All the letters except the big O in Outlook were blue. The O was not an O at all, but a bright orange sun. If it was possible to feel both warm and cold at the same time, I accomplished it.

Where was Chav? I knew in my bones something was wrong. The year we'd spent apart had dulled my psychic ability toward her, so once again I had become inept with crazy flashes that didn't amount to much of anything.

I jiggled the door handle. It wasn't locked, so being the smart, city-savvy girl I am, I decided to let myself in. After all, I owned half the joint, so I wasn't trespassing.

Darkness enclosed the front room except a few areas illuminated by sunlight filtering into the two small windows near the ceiling. They were surrounded by open wooden shutters. Where were the large storefront windows? This place was more dive bar than restaurant. Strange decor choice but my concern for Chav kept me from imagining a complete makeover. I couldn't find a light switch around the door. I should have just gone back out to the truck for a flashlight, but I thought I saw a panel on the wall across the room, and frankly, it was sheer laziness that moved me forward.

I managed to maneuver around the counter, open the panel, and flicked several of the switches at once. The lights came on and when I stepped back to admire my new home lit up—it didn't look half bad; hardwood floors, cute little tables with black-and-white gingham cloth, and a couple of booths with the same checkered design on the benches.

And that's when it happened. My heel caught on something large, and I fell ass-backward to the ground. It didn't take more than a nanosecond to see that I'd tripped over a naked man passed out cold on the floor.

After a startled yelp, heart palpitations, and worry that he'd wake up at any moment and kill me, I reached over and touched him. Just his arm, mind you. He didn't move, but his skin felt warm, and his chest raised and lowered, so I didn't bother to check for a pulse.

Instead, I found myself staring...for several minutes. (Come on. He was naked and lying on his back. Who wouldn't stare?) Dark-brown hair populated his broad chest and led to a happy trail that, well, if the circumstances had been different would have made me very happy indeed. He had thickly muscled thighs and arms, and his face, except for the scruffy five o'clock shadow, looked as if it had been chiseled by Michelangelo. Imagine a better-looking Wolverine (Hugh Jackman's version), but much younger and with a burly lumberjack vibe, and coarse, medium-length walnut-brown hair.

I chewed my lower lip as I took my time pondering the situation—in other words, I wasn't ready to stop staring at the naked man. His hair was near the same hue of brown as my own, when it wasn't dyed blonde, which was never. And mine was shorter with a better haircut. I sighed with regret. I already missed my stylist in California.

Taking a deep breath, I counted backward from ten to pull myself out of the hormonal frenzy going on in my head. The man was hotter than a habanero, but I wasn't looking for a date. I smelled a pungent sweet scent I hadn't noticed before, but frankly I was surprised any of my senses still worked. It was whiskey. Some kind of blended version, if I had to guess.

Great. Just perfect. Burly Hugh looked more and more like a drunk who had crawled into the diner to sleep off a bender.

I found an empty spray bottle by the sink and filled it with water. Positioning myself on the opposite side of the checkout counter (just in case I needed to make a run for it), I leaned over the top and proceeded to spritz the unconscious man. The mist must have been too fine, because other than the rise and fall of his chest, he still didn't move.

Crawling farther up onto the counter, I stretched my arms over the other side, hovering just inches from his face. I pumped the trigger hard three or four times, then screamed and dropped the bottle when his hand shot up and grabbed my wrist. The Neanderthal yanked me completely over the top and onto his naked self. He growled— honest to goodness, I wouldn't lie about such a thing. He growled. The noise started in his chest. I know, because I could feel it in mine, which was now crushed against him.

Why hadn't I just left and called the police? It would have been the easy thing to do—the smart thing. His arms were squeezed tight around me, and I became acutely aware of his Mr. Happy pressing against the skin of my thigh.

His eyelids cracked a peep, then he narrowed his gaze. "Who are you?"

"I..." I should be the one asking the damn questions, but the only ones coming to mind were completely inappropriate. Like, where did he work out? How good looking were his parents to create such a fine specimen of man? And did he have a girlfriend?

There was a moment, a very weak moment on my part, where I began to lower my face to his, our lips only centimeters apart.

*What the hell am I doing?* Where was my head? He could be a serial killer, a rapist, or someone *really* bad, like an Amway salesman. I turned my head away from his.

"Could you let me up, please?"

He squeezed me tighter. "Are you going to answer me?"

Finally, I gulped and squeaked out, "Sunny Haddock."

His left eyebrow rose. "Sunny Haddock?"

"Uh, that would be me. Yes." I'd been in town less than an hour and I was already famous. Well, my name was on the side of the building. "And you would be?"

"Babel Trimmel."

"Chav's baby brother?" I'd heard stories about him, but I'd imagined him to be terminally twelve. The age he'd been when Chav had left Missouri for the West Coast.

"Chavvie made a big mistake. She shouldn't have asked you out here."

Talk about judging someone before you get the know them. Barely through introductions and he already wanted me out. I've made a bad first impression before, but what the fuck? What didn't he like about me? Although maybe it wasn't about like. Because, by the rise of his hoo-ha against my leg, I could swear he liked me a little.

An unfamiliar flutter twittered in my stomach. It'd been awhile since I'd been so physically attracted to anyone. Babel's nostrils flared with a slight huff. His brows narrowed. His eyes dark with purpose. I felt like Little Red Riding Hood, and Babel filled the role of the Big Bad Wolf intent on eating my goody basket. Oh, if only.

*Pull yourself together, Sunny.* But it was really hard, along with his arms, his chest, his abs, his...

Holding me tighter, his arms locked around me. He stroked my back with his firm hands. I trembled, fighting back a deep moan. "Please let me up, Babel," I said again.

He froze for a second then relaxed. He unlocked his arms from around me and smiled. "Call me Babe. Everybody does."

To say I scrambled off his body would be a bit of an overstatement. The trembling had left my arms and knees weak, but I managed, albeit slowly. "I don't know you well enough to call you Babe. Sorry." I couldn't keep my eyes off his semi-erect package.

"Could you put some clothes on? I'm feeling a little..."

He propped up on an elbow like a *Playgirl* centerfold and grinned. "Overdressed?"

*What an egomaniac!* "No. Sheesh." Okay, so maybe I felt a tad overdressed, even in my pink spaghetti-strap shirt dress with black short-shorts and sandals. It was hot in Missouri. Sticky hot. And besides, I'd put in more hours than I care to count at the gym to counterbalance my donut habit, so I deserved to wear those shorts. My exercise routine wasn't all about the donuts. Over a year of no sex, since the dickhead had cheated, and while I'm no sex maniac, that's a long time for someone who had been getting it on the reg.

The "no sex" could also explain why I had such a visceral reaction to this guy. No doubt the man was a hunka-hunka. "Could you quit posing on the floor?" I wagged my finger toward his poker. "And for the love of daisies, put some clothes on before that thing puts out someone's eye."

He had the courtesy to look the tiniest bit embarrassed. "Nothing personal. It's a purely physical reaction."

"I'm sure you say that to all the girls."

"Sorry, I just meant, well, I'm a guy. You brush against the junk, it goes stiff."

"And here I thought I was special." This line of conversation bordered on hurting my feelings. I know I'm not a beauty queen, but neither am I Medusa. "You can shut up now."

Color rose to his cheeks—those nice fuzzy, chiseled, scruffy, manly cheeks, so perfectly bookending his Roman nose and gorgeous bow lips. And damn it to hell, his teeth were friggin' perfect! He pulled himself up by grabbing the counter, and holy schmoly, the man was tall. If I had to guess, he bordered on 6'5". I'm pretty sure I hated him for being so beautifully handsome.

"I only meant to say…"

I almost offered to buy him a shovel, but he managed to dig his own hole quite deep without any help from me. "I've got it already, jeesh. Not interested, physical reaction, yadda, yadda, yadda. No need to explain yourself further. Besides, I'm not looking for a boyfriend, so doesn't matter. And even if I were, it certainly wouldn't be my best friend's baby brother. We cool?" I didn't wait for him to answer. I waved him off. "Great. Excellent. Awesome even. Now, put on some damn clothes." Why-oh-why was I attracted to crazy?

"Perhaps you could find me a diaper."

Guess he didn't like the "baby" comment. Oh well. Sucks to be him.

He covered himself with his hands. Thank God. However, it didn't stop me from checking out the rest of his body. *Ay Chihuahua!* Damn, it kind of sucked to be me.

I knew from Chav that Babel had moved back to

Kansas City where their parents lived after he'd taken a year off from university to look for their brother Judah. What was he still doing here? A horrible thought entered my head. "If you're here, does that mean..."

His face suddenly sobered. "I don't know. Mom and Dad haven't been able to get ahold of her for the last couple of days, so they sent me down to check in. I got here yesterday."

"She texted me a couple of days ago. I haven't been able to get ahold of her since then." I lifted a hand to comfort him, but his nakedness stopped me from breaching the distance. "Babel, we're going to find her." Even if I had to turn over every stump and stone in this backward-ass town.

"Call me Babe. Everyone does."

That was the second time he'd said that to me, but I couldn't call him Babe. No way, no how. Too intimate. Especially since I'd seen him in his birthday suit. "I don't think so."

He chuckled, low and sexy, and everything went right south of my navel. "Sunny,

I'm afraid I've, err...lost my clothes."

"You've got to be kidding me." How did a person go about losing all their damn clothes? "Fine. I'll stay on one side of the counter. You stay on the other. Kapeesh?"

"I understand," he said with a practiced tolerance. It made me wonder who he'd gotten so much practice with.

He hadn't turned around yet, and part of me felt really sad about it. I'm sure he had a killer butt to go with his killer bod. I was all about the teeth and ass. But there were no complaints about the whole frontal part of him either, so…

"Good. Should I call someone for you? Or do you want to call someone? A girlfriend? Anyone who can bring you some clothes?" Subtle. Not.

"The phone's not working here even if I could call someone."

I noticed he'd didn't say "no girlfriend." Much to my annoyance, I cared. And why was the phone turned off? "Don't you have a cell phone that works?"

He moved his hands, indicating his lack of attire. "No pockets."

In the immortal words of Homer Simpson, *Doh*! I snuck another quick glance at his dangly bits, even more annoyed with myself for not having better self-control. "Great. Fantastic." I waved my hand again and purpose-fully looked away. I had a cell phone out in my truck, and was just about to tell him I'd go get it when he stepped out from behind the counter, still full Monty. "Hey! Keep the mammoth covered."

"Flattering. But there's nothing prehistoric about it." He cocked his eyebrow and smirked.

*Bastard.*

"Look here, darling." He pointed to his "junk" as he'd called it and said, "This here is what you call a penis. It's connected to the bladder and the bladder is full. Turn your head if you want, sweetheart, but I'm heading to the john."

"Lovely. And I'm not your darling." I made a show of rolling my eyes and turning away. "I'm going to get my cell phone. I expect you to be standing behind the counter by the time I get back." Now, for the sake of posterity—well, at least for the sake of his posterior—I glanced back as he headed left to the bathroom. Of course, it was sort of hard to notice his ass when I saw the— "Blood..." I whispered.

A pain pierced my temple as my knees buckled beneath me. I dropped to the ground. My peripheral vision narrowed to black. The pounding of blood racing through my arteries swelled loudly in my ears. It was out of beat with my heart.

The thumping of blood stopped, my eyesight began to clear, and I was in Babel's arms.

"Sunny? You okay?" I heard his voice as a muffled echo.

No, I wanted to tell him. I wasn't okay. But my mouth didn't work. A vision came over me. I could sense it like death come knocking. Then I was no longer in Babel's arms. I was a ghost. A spectator.

*I was...in a shabby apartment with furniture dating back to the seventies? Had I traveled to the past? It wasn't unheard of for me, but it couldn't be relevant for something in my life now since I hadn't been born until 1974. Or could it? Great. The powers that be were giving me a psychic reading on my lost Crissy doll. Useless.*

*I heard a muffled cry, maybe a scream from beyond the front door. I passed through and down the stairs. The noise grew louder. Animalistic growls and snarls. Fear tightened in my stomach.*

*It's not real, I reminded myself several times as the feral sounds made me shiver.*

*I couldn't see any creature, but it certainly sounded like someone was getting voraciously attacked. And the room—it looked familiar. Two windows high up on the far wall spilled moonlight across the floor to...the counter? This was the restaurant. The noise continued, loud, animalistic, with grunting, groaning, and a masculine "ah!" Oh. Oh no.*

*If I'd really been there, I'd have run, but the vision took me closer to the scene of the crime. On the floor, behind the counter, a gorgeous woman with long dark hair, golden eyes, and even in the bad lighting, a body I'd give my right tit for, straddled the very naked and very sexy Babel Trimmel. I wanted to gouge out my eyes. Where was a hot poker salesman when you needed him?*

*The woman threw her head back and laughed. "You were fantastic, Babe. As always."*

*He smiled, his eyes rolling back a little. Coming up on his elbows, he leaned his left shoulder forward and looked behind. "You've got to do something about those fingernails."*

*"Just marking my territory."*

*Holy smack, the blood on the floor had happened during sexcapades? Yikes.*

*"I'm not your territory, Sheila."*

*The woman, Sheila apparently, picked up a bottle of Canadian Mist from the floor beside them, took a swig, then dumped some of the amber liquid down his large chest. No wonder the place reeked.*

*Babel shook his head and gave her thigh a light slap. "It's time to go, Sheila. I've got to get the place cleaned up."*

*"You sure you don't want to move here?" She licked his nipple. "I've sure missed you."*

*He sighed. The sigh sounded like it'd been one that he'd perfected over and over for this very argument. "It's not this town or you. I've got a real life out* there.*" He said "there" as though he*

*was talking about an alien planet. "I'm going to find my sister,*
*then get back to it."*

*"And what if you don't find her?" Sheila asked. "You never*
*found Judah."*

*Babel's eyes narrowed. "Not an option," he said. Then added,*
*"I'm finding her, and after, getting the heck out of this town. It's*
*brought nothing but bad luck for my family."*

*"Sorry," she said, as if she wasn't sorry, an evil smile playing*
*on her lips. Okay, so maybe more mischievous than evil, but it*
*was my vision, I could use whatever adjectives I liked. "But you*
*know that answer pisses me off."*

*Before he could blink, she whacked him super hard across the*
*temple with the bottle of blended whiskey, and Babel was out like*
*a light.*

*"Bastard," Sheila muttered. Which I understood, because it*
*had been my sentiment exactly.*

*She dressed quickly, gathered up Babel's clothes, and walked*
*into the kitchen area. It was small, but nice. I hadn't had a chance*
*to see it yet, so it was like my very own psychic tour. She opened*
*the walk-in freezer and chucked the jeans, boots, socks, and T-*
*shirt inside. No underwear. Huh. I'd file that nugget away for*
*later.*

My vision stopped with her slamming the front door,
and suddenly I was back, looking up from the floor at the
towering and still very naked Babel. "Ow." My head, my
back, my butt—everything hurt. "Did you drop me?"

"What the hell just happened?" He looked a little
freaked out.

I got up on my elbows and rubbed the back of my
skull. "Did you drop me on the ground?"

"You were having a seizure or something. I laid you on

the floor." He was definitely freaked. "If I'd had a phone I'd have called for the doc, but..."

"I'm fine now. You can stop worrying." I moved my feet off the chair Babel had propped them up on.

"I'm sorry. I'm squeamish about blood."

Which wasn't a complete lie. Blood tended to bring on funky psychic mojo that left me drained and pained. Although, I'll admit, these visions had been much stronger than normal. Apparently, Chavvah wasn't the only Trimmel who put my psychic stuff on speed dial.

"I'm getting that about you." At least he sounded less upset.

I closed my eyes. "Why would you let someone do that to your back?"

"That's a story for another day, darlin'."

Yeah, I knew the story. Not so sure I wanted the blow-by-blow again. I felt his arms go under me, and I opened my eyes, staring into the deep abyss of his gorgeous, Midwest baby blues.

I let him carry me upstairs to the apartment. I'm not a small woman, but he held me like I weighed next to nothing, which made me think kindlier of him. With my arms around his shoulders, I could smell an unidentifiable musk and spice to his skin. He sat me down on a couch—the scent went from musky to musty—then he went into another room. I heard water running in the sink. More than a whisper of regret passed through me. I barely knew the man and I missed being in his arms. I looked around the living room.

This was the seventies place where my vision had started. The retro decor lacked any sophistication that could've made the space sensational. I knew this had been where Judah lived when he'd been in town. He'd rented this building before his disappearance, and Chav had used our stake to purchase it during her search for him. His vanishing had hit her hard.

Chav told me once that she hadn't agreed with her oldest brother's "lifestyle choice," but she respected him. I'd asked her what she meant, but she had shaken her head, unwilling to elaborate. I knew it wasn't as simple as him being gay or anything like that, because Chav, like myself, was socially liberal. Hell, she'd have started her own PFLAG (Parents, Families, and Friends of Lesbians and Gays) in Peculiar if that had been the case. No. There was something else she hadn't approved of.

I heard the water turn off in the kitchen. Babel returned and proceeded to wipe my face and neck with a cool cloth.

"There now, all better." For a second, he sounded like my father. Which totally squicked me, considering the hard-core fantasies I had about him. He put the wash-cloth in my hand and patted my shoulder. "I'm going to jump in the shower real quick. I'll be back in a few."

Part of me wanted to watch him walk away strictly for the view, but since that part seemed to have done gone and lost its damn mind, I waited until I heard water running before looking in his direction.

He'd left the bathroom door open. Perv.

I couldn't believe it, less than an hour in a new town and I'd witnessed a *Red Shoe Diary* moment, and the star was lathering up less than ten feet away. I would've been downright disgusted by the whole morning if I hadn't been so preoccupied with thoughts of slippery suds sliding along his perfectly formed pecs. (Now I understand how bad porn gets started. Bow chick-a bow-wow.)

*I will not go stare at the naked man.* I repeated this mantra in my head over and over as I ran down the stairs to the kitchen.

Grabbing his clothes from the freezer, I contemplated where they'd been and how they got there as I carried them back upstairs. They were cold and held the scent of sweat, but at least he'd have something to put on so he could go away. I placed them on the couch, and dear Lord, it was a really ugly couch. It would be the first piece of furniture to go when Chav and I started fixing the place up. And with that thought, I went downstairs to wait for him.

Fifteen minutes later, the light flickered on in the stairwell. Babel's arms and face glistened with dewy goodness as he walked down the steps. He rubbed a tea towel, barely big enough to dry a fish's butt, against his loose mane of wet hair. His blue T-shirt clung to his chest. Water soaking through the fabric made spots the color of midnight.

He must have felt me staring, because he dropped his arm to his side and looked at me. "Where'd you find my clothes?"

"The freezer." I wrapped my knuckle on the counter. "Guess you can go home now."

"Guess so." He shrugged as he stretched his body to tuck in his shirt. "But we should probably talk."

"I'm in no mood." *For talk.* Damn, he was super-fine.

"Well, you kind of need to get in the mood." He shook

his hair out, droplets spraying out around him. It began to feel like a bad (or really good, depending on who you asked) shampoo commercial. "There's been a mistake. My sister should've never invited you out here, Sunny."

"You've said that already, but unfortunately for you, my name's on the property, same as hers, all legal and binding. I'm staying. Period. End of discussion. Besides, I'm not going anywhere until I find Chav."

Babel chewed his lower lip and narrowed his eyes at me. "I don't think you understand the situation."

"Oh, I think I do. You don't like me. Fine. I get that."

"It's a might more complicated than that." He scratched at his five o'clock shadow.

I resisted the temptation to offer him a hand. "Why do you care, anyway? Don't you have a *real* life you want to get back to? You seem awfully concerned for a guy who isn't even sticking around."

"And what makes you think that?" Babel asked.

"Uh..." Fair question. I couldn't exactly tell him that I'd heard him tell his cuh-razy lover in a vision. "Well, you didn't exactly stick around after the search was called off for Judah."

A pained expression crossed his face. I instantly regretted being such an ass. It was a low blow, and petty even.

"I stayed for as long as I could stand it." He shook his head. "I'm not meant for this place, Sunny. And neither are you."

Another twinge. "It doesn't matter." We would find Chavvah, then he would be gone. "Have you heard anything? Are the police searching for her?"

"No and yes. I haven't heard from Chavvie, but Sheriff Taylor isn't giving up." He flicked his thumbnail against his ring fingernail. "Not yet, anyways."

"She'll show up, Babel. I just know it." But I didn't know it. In my heart, I believed she was alive, and not because of any vision. "She's my best friend. I'd feel it if she was gone. Now, go on back to wherever you're staying..." Oh, crap. Maybe he'd been staying here. "You do have another place to stay don't you?"

Babel nodded once. "I've been staying at Chavvie's cabin down by the lake."

"Good," I whispered. I'd want to check out her place later for clues to what happened. "It's been a long drive for me, and I need a nap so I can figure out what I have to do next to find her."

He shook his head as if he was having an argument with himself. "I'll be back in a couple of hours with some cleaning supplies and get the floor behind the counter scrubbed."

I didn't want to talk anymore. I wanted to get my bags out of the truck. I'd hassle with unpacking the U-Haul later, but the bags were a must. I needed something personal, something of mine in this place. I held out my hand. "That's a nice offer. I can manage. Thanks."

Babel took my hand, and gave me a tight-lipped smile. "You don't handle blood very well. After I clean it up, maybe we can compare notes about Chavvie."

I nodded, afraid that if I spoke the dams would open and I wouldn't be able to stop the tears. Then I heard a voice like a whisper in my ear.

*Save her.*

Babel let go of my hand. "I'll be back." The way he said it sounded more like a threat than a promise. As he walked out the front door, he added, "You've got an audience."

**Get this book from your favorite eTailer!**

# PARANORMAL MYSTERIES & ROMANCES

## BY RENEE GEORGE

**Grimoires of a Middle-aged Witch**
Earth Spells Are Easy (Book 1)
Spell On Fire (Book 2)
When the Spells Blows (Book 3)
Spell Over Troubled Water (Book 4)
Ghost in the Spell (Book 5)

**Peculiar Mysteries & Romances**
You've Got Tail (Book 1)
My Furry Valentine (Book 2)
Thank You For Not Shifting (Book 3)
My Hairy Halloween (Book 4)
In the Midnight Howl (Book 5)
Furred Lines (Book 6)
My Wolfy Wedding (Book 7)
Who Let The Wolves Out? (Book 8)
My Thanksgiving Faux Paw (Book 9)

**Nora Black Midlife Psychic Mysteries**

Sense & Scent Ability (Book 1)

For Whom the Smell Tolls (Book 2)

War of the Noses (Book 3)

Aroma With A View (Book 4)

Spice and Prejudice (Book 5)

Age of Inno-Scents (Book 6)

Aroma Holiday (Book 7)

**Witchin' Impossible Paranormal Mysteries**

Witchin' Impossible (Book 1)

Rogue Coven (Book 2)

Familiar Protocol (Booke 3)

Mr & Mrs. Shift (Book 4)

**Barkside of the Moon Paranormal Mysteries**

Pit Perfect Murder (Book 1)

Murder & The Money Pit (Book 2)

The Pit List Murders (Book 3)

Pit & Miss Murder (Book 4)

The Prune Pit Murder (Book 5)

Two Pits and A Little Murder (Book 6)

Pits and Pieces of Murder (Book 7)

**Hex Drive**

Hex Me, Baby, One More Time (Book 1)

Oops, I Hexed It Again (Book 2)

I Want Your Hex (Book 3)

Hex Me With Your Best Shot (Book 4)

Hex Me All Night Long (Book 5)

**Madder Than Hell**

Gone With The Minion (Book 1)
Devil On A Hot Tin Roof (Book 2)
A Street Car Named Demonic (Book 3)

# SENSE AND SCENT ABILITY

## A NORA BLACK MIDLIFE PSYCHIC
## MYSTERY BOOK 1

## Chapter One

"I think I have a brain tumor," I blurted as I flung open my front door for my best friend, Gillian "Gilly" Martin. She held a bottle of wine in one hand and a grocery bag filled with honey buns, potato chips, salted nuts, and chocolate-covered raisins in her other.

"You don't have a brain tumor." Gilly passed off the bag and the bottle, then brushed past me, shrugging off her coat and hanging it on the hall tree. It had been a cold March, with temperatures in the low 40s most days. Under the coat, Gilly wore a form-fitting, long-sleeved, baby blue turtleneck sweater and black palazzo pants that flared out over a pair of black flats. Her straight chestnut-brown hair was in a loose ponytail for our girls' night in.

"Are you pooping okay?" she asked. "The doctor said you weren't supposed to strain. You could pop internal stitches."

"Quit asking me about my bowel habits," I said. "As of

yesterday, I've been cleared to resume normal activity. Like straining when I poop. Besides, I'm worried about my head, not my butt." After all, my mother had died of brain cancer. "I've been… " I trailed off, trying to find the right words. "Seeing things."

Gilly squeezed my shoulder in an effort to comfort me. "You had a hysterectomy, Nora. Didn't the doctor say you might feel strange for a while?"

Um…if strange included dying on the operating table and then discovering strong scent-induced hallucinations, then yeah. I felt strange. I mean if death was gonna bring me a gift, I would've liked something a lot more useful than the ability to smell other people's troubles.

How could I possibly explain my new weird ability to her? Well, obviously, I couldn't. It had been eight weeks since my surgery, and I still hadn't figured out a way to confide in Gilly.

"Nora?"

I sighed. "I need a drink." I lifted up the wine bottle. "Let me pop this sucker." Gilly still looked concerned, but I smiled and nodded toward the living room. "Be right there."

A few minutes later, I handed Gilly her glass of Cabernet Sauvignon and sat down next to her on the couch.

"You know, regular activities include sex," Gilly said with a little too much enthusiasm. She waggled her brows at me.

"Sex hasn't been a regular activity for me in a very long time." Two years to be exact. I wasn't a prude. It's just that there hadn't been a lot of opportunities. Between caring for my mother during the last stages of her illness and dealing with painful uterine fibroids, dating and sex were the last things I cared about.

"You are way too hot to be celibate."

"Sure." I patted my swelly-belly. "I've gained ten pounds in the last two months."

"You just had your guts cut out," she said with a fair amount of exasperation. Then she flashed me her signature Gilly Martin smile, and added, "Besides, men like women with curves."

I frowned and pinched some of my stomach fat. "It's too squishy to be a curve."

She laughed. "Girl. I got squishy curves all over." She rubbed her tummy. "Including my midsection." She fluffed her ponytail. "And I'm sexy as hell."

I grinned. "You certainly are." I had always lacked the confidence Gilly displayed about her looks and body. She wasn't wrong about her sex appeal. Men were drawn to her like bears to honey.

"Have I told you lately how happy I am that you're back in Garden Cove?"

I rolled my eyes then grinned. "All the time."

"I can't help it. I missed you when you lived in the city." Her sigh held a hint of sadness. "Though, I'm sorry for the reason you had to come home."

Last year, my mother's brain cancer had progressed to its final stage. My father had died ten years ago, and I was an only child. Mom only had me. So, I'd taken a compassionate leave of absence from work as a regional sales manager for a prominent health and beauty line to care for her. It had turned into an early retirement when my employer decided they wanted to keep my temporary replacement, a younger, more cutthroat version of myself. Thankfully, they'd offered me a generous severance package if I would go quietly, including covering medical insurance costs until I qualified for Medicare in fourteen years.

I'd accepted their offer. Spending time with Mom until her final moments had been a blessing. I didn't regret a minute of caring for her. Of course, from the hospice workers, the aides, the nurses, the volunteers who would sit with her while I shopped, and even the chaplain who brought her some spiritual comfort, I hadn't done it alone.

My mother had been the rock of our family, a major source of comfort and stability. When she got sick, she'd minimized the severity of her cancer because she hadn't wanted me to worry. Honestly, I'd believed she'd beat it. I'd never seen Mom not succeed when she put her mind to something. If only I had known how bad it really was, I would have come home sooner.

Reconnecting with Gilly had been one of the major bright spots since moving back to Garden Cove. We'd been inseparable during elementary and high school. She'd been the maid of honor at my wedding and had done the pub crawl up in the city with me when my divorce had finalized. I had been twenty-nine at the time. It was hard to believe that twenty-two years had passed since then. When I was in my teens, I couldn't wait for high school to be over so I could make my own life. Then in college, I couldn't wait to graduate so I could be married. Later, when my marriage fell apart, I couldn't wait to be out of it so I could move away from Garden Cove and start my career.

I'd spent so much time wishing my life away that I'd failed to really live in the moment. I didn't want to be that person anymore.

My whole life had been go-go-go, and I was ready for some slow-slow-slow.

I squeezed Gilly's hand. "I missed you, too. You know, it's not too late to quit your job and come work with me in the shop."

Gilly smiled. "I like running the spa at the Rose Palace Resort."

"I know you do." I didn't press her. We'd had this conversation a dozen times since I'd bought Tidwell's Diner and converted it into an apothecary, where I sold homemade beauty and aromatherapy products. I couldn't afford to pay her what she was worth, anyhow. But it didn't stop me from wishing we could spend more time together. I considered myself lucky that she'd had tonight free.

Gilly was a single mom to teenage twins, and the high school was out for their short spring break that would end on Monday and Tuesday thanks to snow days in January that they still had to make up. The kids were doing overnights at their friends, while Gilly had packed a bag to stay in my guest bedroom and leave for work in the morning from here. Hence the wine. "How are the kids doing?"

"Like they would tell me." Gilly snorted. "They're teenagers, so they share as little as possible. Marco seems to be doing okay. He's dating a girl a year older than him.

A senior. Can you believe it? I wouldn't have ever dated a younger boy in high school."

"Marco's a good-looking kid."

"He's only sixteen and just like his dad," Gilly agreed. "Oozing charm and confidence. Worries me sometimes."

"He's not anything like Gio," I assured her. Marco, while moody and temperamental at times, had a kind heart, unlike his father, who only cared about himself. The twins never saw their dad anymore, and that was on Giovanni Rossi. After the divorce, he took a head chef position at an Italian restaurant in Vegas. He used his work as a way to avoid parental responsibility. Too often, Gilly carried that burden of guilt, as if it was her fault Gio had abandoned his kids.

"What about Ari?" I asked.

"She made the honor roll." Gilly's daughter's full name was Ariana Luna Isabelle Rossi. A beautiful name, but she preferred Ari. The girl marched to the beat of her own drum, and I loved that about her. Where her mother was hyper-feminine in both hair and clothes, Ari wore her hair like James Dean, and her outfits tended to be androgynous. "She's so smart, but I can't help but worry about her. She's so damned quiet. How in the world did I, a woman who can't shut up, raise a daughter who doesn't like to talk?"

"You got me there," I said, offering a sly smirk.

"Nora!" She smacked my arm. "You're terrible."

"Ouch." I rubbed the spot and laughed. "I really am. Good for Ari, though," I said. "She's always been a smart cookie. And her drive and ambition to excel will take her places." I didn't have children by choice, but that hadn't stopped me from agreeing to be Marco and Ari's godmother. When I lived in the city, I'd sent the kids packages every year for birthdays and Christmas, but I hadn't spent a lot of time with them until I returned to Garden Cove. "She's going to be just fine, even if she didn't inherit her mother's gift of gab." I slung my arm around Gilly's shoulders and squeezed, careful not to jostle our wine glasses.

I caught the sweet scent of raspberries with notes of citrus and vanilla.

*Blurry shapes form...a woman stands in front of a large man who towers over her. Faces are hazy. It appears as if they're both made of colored smoke.*

*"It's over, Lloyd."*

*I recognize Gilly's voice.*

*"Don't be that way, Gilly," the man cajoles. "I didn't mean anything by it."*

*Gilly's voice chokes. "I really like you, but I can't be with someone who would say those things. Especially about my daughter. Ari is a great kid."*

*She turns away from him and he grabs her arm. Gilly gasps as he yanks her against his body.*

*"We belong together." He manacles both her wrists with his large hands. "You have to give me another chance."*

*"Get your hands off me," she says, pain evident in her shaking voice.*

*"I'll never let you go." His menacing tone chills me to the bone. "Never."*

"Hello." Gilly snapped her fingers in front of my face. "Earth to Nora."

"What?" I said, blinking at my friend.

Her brow furrowed. "Are you okay?"

"You're going to get grooves between your eyes if you don't stop worrying about me." Although, at this point, I had enough worry for the both of us." "How is it going with the new guy you're dating? Lloyd Briscoll, right?"

Gilly went pale and the wine glass in her hand trembled. I took it from her, then placed both of our glasses on the coffee table. "Gilly?"

"I'm fine," she said, her voice pitched to an unbelievably cheery tone. "Didn't you promise me a date with Mr. Darcy?"

I'd wanted to tell her about my scent-stimulated hallucinations, and maybe now was the time. This was the first...er, vision I'd had about my best friend. Still...what if I was wrong? If I really did have a brain tumor, and these experiences were a symptom of being sick, then it would be stupid to worry Gilly. Besides, if she thought I was nuts, she might decide to tie me up, throw me in the car, and take me to the nearest emergency room.

But her avoidance of my question, in addition to the vision, stirred a bad feeling in the pit of my stomach.

"Tell me what's going on," I said softly.

Gilly took a sudden interest in a loose stitch at the bottom of her sweater, tugging on it to avoid my gaze. "We broke up." She paused. "Correction. I broke up with him." Gilly pushed up the cuff of her sleeve and revealed finger-sized bruises on her wrist.

"He did this?" I asked. My stomach clenched. What I'd glimpsed of Gilly and Lloyd's interaction had been real. Holy crap. Without thinking, I asked, "Was it something to do with Ari?"

Gilly gave me a sharp look. "How did you..." She shook her head then nodded. "I overheard him laughing with some of his buddies in the security office." Her hands were shaking now, and there was anger in her voice. "They were talking about Ari." Her eyes narrowed as her ire surfaced. "He called Ari a freak, and some other unsavory slurs that I won't repeat, because she happens to wear her hair short and the way she dresses."

I took her hand and gave it a pat. "He's an asshole."

"I marched right into that room gave him the it's-not-me-it's-definitely-you speech. He grabbed me and told me we were done when he said we were done."

"Is that after he told you he'd never let you go?"

Gilly paled. "Yes. How did you know that?"

Alarm kicked my adrenaline in. I skipped her question and went right to the important part. "That's a threat, Gilly. You need to call the police."

"And tell them what? Who's going to believe Silly Gilly over the head of security for the Rose Palace? Lloyd is an ex-cop, and he still has a lot of friends on the force."

"Yeah? Well, so do I."

"You mean your ex-husband chief of police who you haven't spoken to in ten years? That guy?" Gilly scoffed. "Shawn Rafferty didn't like me when you two were married."

Shawn and I had divorced for a myriad of reasons, but mostly because he'd changed his mind about wanting kids. I had not. When we divorced, we split everything down the middle, and since we didn't have children and we were both just starting our lives, I didn't sue for alimony. I didn't want anything tying us together anymore. Not even a last name, so I took back my maiden name. And then poof, like magic, it had been as if the five years we were married and the four years we dated never existed.

But say what you want about my ex-husband, he's a good cop. And, yeah, a good person. He and his wife had sent a lovely spray of lilies for my mom's funeral, and Shawn had even stopped in at the visitation. Our conversation, the first one we'd had since my dad had died a decade ago, had been short but not unpleasant.

"Shawn will believe you." I clasped both of her hands and looked her in the eye. "Promise me you'll call the police if that son-of-a-bitch comes within fifty feet of you again."

"We both work at the Rose Palace. Our paths are bound to cross." Gilly blew out a breath. "But I'll do my best to avoid him."

I stared at her hard, my mouth set in a grim line.

She raised her hand as if taking an oath. "And I'll call the police if he attempts to even talk to me." She pushed my shoulder lightly. "Now, come on. I didn't come over here to lament my tragic taste in men. You promised me a night of binge-watching Jane Austen movies, good wine, and all the popcorn I can eat."

My smile felt tight. Gilly was an adult, and she'd been living her life just fine for many years without me telling her what to do. "You're absolutely right. Let's fill up these wine glasses, and I'll start the popcorn. You break out the goodies." Like a weirdo, I loved mixing chocolate-covered raisins in with my salty popcorn. Yum.

Twenty minutes later, we were sitting on my comfy couch with throw blankets over our legs, a large popcorn bowl between us and honey buns on the coffee table. Our wine glasses were full of Cabernet Sauvignon, and our undivided attention was on Mr. Darcy.

"Why can't real men be like him?" Gilly bemoaned after Darcy gave Elizabeth moon eyes.

"No, thank you," I told her. "I like the fantasy of Darcy, but he's judgy and bossy and arrogant. Give me a guy who is genuinely interested in my happiness, and not what he *thinks* will make me happy. That's the guy I'll spend the rest of my life with." Not that I thought such a man existed. I wasn't content exactly, but I was resigned to living out my life as a single woman. I glanced at Gilly. At least, I knew I'd never be alone. Not with friends like her in my life. I nudged her and smiled. "Even so, I'll happily root for Elizabeth Bennet to get her man."

"So, you are looking for a man," Gilly said triumphantly.

"You're the worst," I said.

Gilly made a kissy face in my direction. "Best Bitches Forever."

High-beam headlights glared through my living room window. I shielded my eyes and waited for them to go off. They didn't.

"Who is that?" Gilly asked. "Were you expecting anyone?"

"No. Just you." I got up and looked outside with Gilly right behind me.

"Oh. Oh, no," she hissed. "It's Lloyd."

"Go lock the front door," I said. When she didn't move, I said with more force, "Now!"

Gilly took off toward the front door, and I moved

quickly up the stairs to my bedroom, ignoring my creaky knees as I retrieved my gun case from my bedside table. My hands were trembling as I opened the case and grabbed my compact 9mm and a full clip of bullets. I loaded the gun while I returned to the front of the house.

It was dark outside. "Is he still out there?" I asked.

"Gilly!" I heard a man shout. "Gilly, come talk to me. I just want to talk. I'm sorry about earlier. I didn't mean it. I swear. I promise it won't happen again."

Gilly had her body pressed against the wall and out of sight. "I think he turned off the light so he could see inside," she said. "He won't stop calling for me."

"How did he know you were here?" An awful thought occurred to me. "The kids?"

"No," she said. "They're staying the night with friends." She shook her head. "I told him a couple of days ago that I was coming over here to celebrate your recovery." Her pitch went up a notch as tears flooded her eyes. "I'm so stupid."

"He's stupid. Not you."

"Gilly!" he bellowed. "Come out and talk to me. Don't make me come in there after you."

"That is just about enough." I loaded a round into the chamber of my pistol and stalked to the door. "Call the police," I said.

"I already did," she said. "What are you going to do?"

"I'm going to get that jerk off my property."

I unlocked and opened the front door, walking out with my weapon extended in front of me. The wind whipped my hair across my face, and I pushed it back with my free hand. I hadn't bothered to put on shoes, and the rough concrete from my walk bit into my socked feet. I ignored the discomfort as I took aim at the drunk in my driveway.

Lloyd, a tall man, handsome, even with a receding hairline, gave me a look of sheer incredulity. He wore a dark nylon jacket with a tear in the pocket, his cheek was red and swollen, and his lip was bleeding. I guessed this wasn't the first fight he'd started tonight.

"Get back in your car and leave, Lloyd. And stay away from Gilly," I said. "The police are on their way, and if you're gone before they get here, I won't file a complaint."

"You can't shoot me." He laughed. "Castle law means I have to be in the place you live. Otherwise, you'll go to jail for assault or attempted murder."

"The way I see it, I can shoot you, then Gilly and I can drag you into the house."

He walked up to me and pressed his chest against the barrel of my gun. "Go ahead, tough girl. Shoot me."

The sour scent of beer mixed with whiskey made my stomach roil.

*I recognize his out-of-focus form before the reek of booze confirms it. "Bitch!" Lloyd yells. He grabs a red-haired woman, his hands encircling her throat. Like Lloyd, I can't make out her face, and with her knees buckled, I can't tell how tall or short she might be, but I can feel her desperation. She struggles to escape but he is too strong.*

*"Please," she whispers, barely audible. "You're...choking...me."*

*He throws her to the ground and straddles her, his thick hands squeezing her throat. But who's his victim? I'm helpless. She's dying. He's killing her.*

I snapped out of it, full of rage. I lifted the 9mm

higher and aimed at Lloyd's head. Something in my eyes must have frightened him because he took several steps back.

Sirens sang out in the distance.

"Tick-tock," I said to Lloyd. "A smart man would already be in his car."

He scowled at me. "Crazy bitch." On that note, he jumped into his vehicle, started it up, and squealed his tires as he reversed out of the driveway.

Gilly came running outside clasping a butcher knife. "Oh my gosh, Nora. You're a freaking superhero."

"When the police arrive, I'm filing a report," I said, trying not to pass out.

She whipped the knife around in the air. "But you told Lloyd—"

"Gilly, stop waving that thing before you hurt yourself."

She blushed as she dropped her arm to her side. "I forgot I was holding it. What are we going to say to the police?"

"The truth. Lloyd Briscoll is a bad guy, Gilly. Like, really bad." I shivered as pieces of the vision played in my head. "He needs to be reported. And you need to show them your bruises. I have a feeling this man isn't going to leave you alone without encouragement."

**Click Here to Keep Reading!**

# PRAISE FOR RENEE GEORGE

"Grimoires of a Middle Aged Witch is my new favorite series! I want a gnome named Linda of my own. Trust me. Read the series. You will not regret a single delightfully hilarious and heartwarming moment.

*- Robyn Peterman, NYT and USA Today Bestselling Author of Good to the Last Death series.*

"I love Renee's books, and recommend any of her series! They catch me right up and keep me turning those pages."

*-Yasmine Galenorn, New York Times Bestselling Author*

"Renee George has crafted a fantastic start to this magical midlife adventure. Pick up Earth Spells Are Easy today! You won't be disappointed."

*-Dakota Cassidy, USA Today Bestselling Author*

"I'm loving the Paranormal Women's Fiction genre! Renee George's humor shines when a woman of a certain age sniffs out the bad guy and saves her bestie. Funny, strong female friendships rule!"

*-- Michelle M. Pillow, NYT & USAT Bestselling Author*

# ABOUT THE AUTHOR

I am a USA Today Bestselling author who writes paranormal mysteries and romances because I love all things whodunit, Otherworldly, and weird. Also, I wish my pittie, the adorable Kona Princess Warrior and my two cats Ash and Simon could talk. Or at least be more like Scooby-Doo and help me unmask villains at the haunted house up the street.

When I'm not writing about mystery-solving were-cougars or the adventures of a hapless psychic living among shapeshifters, I am preyed upon by stray kittens who end up living in my house because I can't say no to those sweet, furry faces. (Someone stop telling them where I live!)

I live in Mid-Missouri with my family and I spend my non-writing time doing really cool stuff...like watching TV and cleaning up dog poop

### Follow Renee!
Bookbub
Renee's Rebel Readers FB Group
Newsletter

www.ingramcontent.com/pod-product-compliance
Lightning Source LLC
Chambersburg PA
CBHW030248200626
46816CB00002BA/551